SHARON MIERKE

MW01138040

Return to Sarah's Valley

By

Sharon Mierke

SHARON MIERKE

Copyright 2017 by Sharon Mierke

THE RETURN TO SARAH'S VALLEY

Return to Sarah's Valley is a follow-up story to *Sarah's Valley,* which was published in 2012 by the same author, Sharon Mierke.

In *Sarah's Valley*, Patrick Smithson meets Frank Lawdry, an elderly man who lives in the Qu'Appelle Valley in southern Saskatchewan, Canada. Frank, who prefers his Abenaki name, Winnipesaukee, spends the night recalling his life story. He and his sister, Sarah, were left orphans when everyone on a wagon train, traveling from the east coast of the United States to California, died in a horrific tragedy. It was their story of survival.

Return to Sarah's Valley continues where *Sarah's Valley* leaves off. Now an old man in his nineties, Patrick meets Michael Lawdry, one of Winnipesaukee's descendants, and tells him how two Lawdry men influenced his life. This is a story of life during the Great Depression, struggles and heartache, but also the deep love that a man has for one woman.

Sharon Mierke writes historical fiction (*Sarah's Valley, Return to Sarah's Valley, and The Widow's Walk*) and cozy mysteries. She has two mystery series: The Mabel Wickles series (*Deception by Design, Calamity by the Car Wash, Cold Case Conundrum, and Frozen Identity*) and the Beryl Swallows series (*Virtual Enemies, Case Closed.not*).

 You can connect with Sharon on Facebook, Twitter, and Instagram.

Return to Sarah's Valley is dedicated to my two editors, Val and Elfie; my two cover designers, Natasha and Justin, and my publisher, Al. Thank you so much for all your time and patience.

SHARON MIERKE

Return to Sarah's Valley

*T*he icy wind beat against the old man's back making it impossible to straighten up so he stayed bent over, moving with the current, and keeping his eyes to the ground. His gray woolen coat clung to the back of his legs and his scarf whipped across his face. It was the end of November and he knew it was the last time he would be walking out to Molly's grave. Even this morning, the staff at the Home was not too pleased but he insisted that he was going, with or without a companion or their permission.

"Why do you insist on making this into a prison?" he asked the Director of the Home. "You know how important *this is to me. You know that I have to go. This will probably be my last visit before spring."*

Karen Freeman had stopped arguing with Patrick Smithson many years before. Or, had tried to. He could be stubborn and cantankerous but at the same time, she couldn't help but respect the elderly resident. How many men would remain so faithful to one woman after all these years? Her husband hadn't remained faithful for even three years.

She usually lost most arguments with him so her strategy was to try to put a guilt trip on him.

"Patrick," she said, "You're welcome to visit your wife's grave any time. However, because there's a winter storm on the way, you'll have to have a companion. You know very well that if something happens to you out there, I'm the one who's going to get blamed. I'm the one whose job is always on the line." She glared at the old man. "Am I understood?"

He shook his head and let out a heaving sigh. What did she think he was? A child?

"I believe I understand English, Karen, but I doubt your job is at risk. You're exaggerating."

"Right, Patrick, as if you would know."

She turned towards one of the staff in the hallway who was making a feeble attempt at trying to look busy and yelled her name.

"Andrea!"

Patrick wondered if this was a coincidence, or was Karen doing this on purpose. She knew Patrick had his favorites but this girl was definitely not one of them.

Patrick rolled his eyes but suppressed another sigh. He watched as she turned her back to him and entered the hole-in-the-wall room she called her office. Which, he was sure was the reason she was always in such a miserable mood. A room without windows was as close to a dungeon as you could get. Or, perhaps it was her love life, or lack thereof, that make her cranky.

Not that the companion she chose could be of much help. He wasn't quite sure what talents or skills the girl possessed. It wouldn't have surprised him if she was a school dropout. She had started working on his wing of the building two weeks before. He noticed that every time she thought no one was watching, she was on her cell phone. Even now, he knew that if he glanced back, she would be either standing or walking, looking down at that fixation. In many ways, he was glad he wouldn't live long enough to see what sort of mess her generation was going to leave behind. He had already lived long enough to see how much the world had changed in his lifetime. Oh yes, there was much progress in many fields of science and technology but not much advancement in human kindness and empathy.

Large fluffy flakes were descending from the heavens now, swirling aimlessly with each burst of wind. Small drifts were beginning to form against concrete curbs and tufts of dead grass. Patrick often wondered why anyone lived in this godforsaken part of the world. In the winter, the wind swept across the prairies, frigid and merciless. Over the years, he knew of several who had lost their way in a blizzard and froze to death. In summer, the blazing sun beat down on the dried-up prairie grass and whatever had been green in late spring was now brown and dead. Why had he stayed all these years?

Well, he knew. He could never go too far from Molly.

Molly's grave was in the far northwest section of the graveyard. There hadn't been that many gravestones back when her father buried her but now he had to pass by rows and rows before coming to hers. It wasn't only her gravesite. She shared that spot with someone else. He always had mixed feelings when he stood and looked down at the small marker. There was no name, no date of birth or death. It read only Baby as if the tiny individual who lay beneath the ground had never existed. But to Patrick it was someone, even though he had entered Patrick's life for only an instant and then was gone forever. All he really remembered was the perfectly formed tiny body and the bluish-white skin. This color because there had been no life *in him when he came into the world. And not long afterwards, there was no life left in Molly either. Molly and their child both died that day. That was the day something inside Patrick died too.*

Molly was not quite seventeen years old. She was but a child herself and yet at the time, they both felt they were so mature, so sure of their future. Their love knew no bounds.

He never forgave himself for allowing this to happen and sadly, neither did Molly's father. The cabin where he and Molly lived together for such a brief time was no longer his home. Within hours of the tragedy, Jacob Jordan forced him to leave with as many of his belongings as he could shove into a small suitcase. He never wanted to see his son-in-law again ... at least, not alive. Folks came from the surrounding area to pay their respects to the family while he, the husband, went into hiding. Two days after Molly's funeral, which Patrick was unable to attend, his father-in-law set fire to the little log house as if that would erase the memory of his daughter's death. It was so long ago now but to Patrick, it was a memory that could have happened yesterday.

The old man reached his wife's gravestone and held on to it. He always did when he came to see her. It somehow made him feel bonded to her. A bond that even death could not sever. The stone felt like a block of ice and he could feel the cold penetrating through his mitt.

"Well, good morning, Molly, sweetheart," he said, in a quiet voice. After saying this, he glanced back at his companion but when he saw she was still back at the graveyard entrance talking on her phone, he continued, "This will be my last visit before the real winter sets in. They say an early winter storm is heading our way so I won't be staying long. Maybe I'll come back in the spring. It's hard to say. You know, I'm ninety-five years old now, Molly. Remember how we promised that we would grow old together? And here I am, growing old all by myself." He laughed. "No, not growing old, my love, I am old." He brushed the first tear from his cheek with his hand. "I know you wouldn't like living where I live now. It's only a place for dying elderly people. I do wish you were with me though." He stopped speaking as his tears gently travelled down his face, following the crevices in his aged skin. Patrick pulled a cotton handkerchief from his jacket pocket to wipe his cheeks and blow his nose.

He straightened up and looked back again. Andrea was still on her phone. Her sudden shrill burst of laughter filled the still cold air. Even from that far away, it irritated him.

He could remember the days when he was a young man and was able to come here by himself. When she first died, he used to come after dark so no one would see him. Molly's father threatened he would shoot him on sight so Patrick moved away to find work on another farm. Most folks thought he would leave for some faraway place, never to return but he would never leave Molly. Every weekend he would drive over, park about a half mile away, and sneak into the graveyard. That was all he had of her except for two small pictures taken on their wedding day by a stranger.

*"I knew what it meant to have a broken heart, Molly,"
he said. "You can't even imagine how I ached to have you back with me. All these years have passed now but you will always be my first and only true love." He looked down at the gravestone and the words engraved there. "Your father had those words put on the headstone. Words that didn't include me. He didn't even acknowledge your married name. I know you can't see it, Molly, but it only reads, 'Beloved Daughter of Martha and Jacob Jordan' - not 'Beloved Wife of Patrick Smithson.' Well, I guess I've complained about that to you many times before. Those words nearly ripped my heart out but what could I do?" He shook his head. "I was only a lad and didn't know how to stand up for myself."*

"Are you ready to go? I'm freezing here," Andrea bellowed, as she stomped her feet.

"Well, old girl, I hear my companion calling me so I better go. These workers at the nursing home don't have much tolerance nowadays. I guess we move too slowly for them. There's so much we could tell them about life but they don't have the patience to sit and listen."

"You hear me, Patrick?" she screamed. "It's time to go."

He gave the marble headstone another pat.

"That will be all for today, Molly. I hope I get to come out again but I can't promise anything. Just remember you are always in my heart, my darling."

He turned to see Andrea marching towards him. The wind was picking up and the girl wore only a short jacket with no scarf or gloves. Her long dark hair blew across her face and she angrily tried to put it behind her ears.

"This was a stupid thing to do, you know," she said. "I'll probably end up sick as a dog now." She held onto his arm and tried to force him to walk faster. "Why did you have to come out on a day like this anyway?"

Patrick kept silent. There was no point in trying to explain to a young woman, who obviously had never suffered any sort of loss in her life, that this might be his last visit before the gravediggers dug a hole for him. Her biggest loss, he thought, would be if she ever lost her cell phone. The thought of that brought a smile to his face and a bit of mischief to his mind. He quickened his pace.

As soon as they walked through the front doors of the Home, Karen stood, hands on hip, waiting for them. By the look on her face, she had been waiting longer than she had cared to.

"Patrick," she said, "You need to have a quick lunch because you have company coming in about an hour. I *should never have agreed to let you go out in this weather. If I'd known you were going to keep Andrea away so long, I wouldn't have let you go." She shook her head as if it was her fault but trying harder to make Patrick feel guilty.*

Even if it were a warm sunny day, the reaction was always the same: "What took you so long, Patrick?" He often wondered what they thought he should do - walk up to the gravestone to see if it was still standing and then leave?

Patrick took his mitts off and started working on his scarf.

"What do you mean that I have company coming?"

Karen started unbuttoning his jacket.

"I'm not sure who it is. He said his name was Lawdry or something like that."

The old man stopped and stared at her. "His name was Lawdry? Are you sure?"

She grabbed his scarf and mittens and started stuffing them into his jacket pockets.

"Yes, I'm sure. What is he? Your lawyer?"

He smiled. "No, but it's a name I knew from many years ago."

Karen's eyebrows went up. "Really?"

He nodded. "Many many years ago. The first time was when I was sixteen years old. I met an old man whose name was Frank Lawdry but he called himself Winnipesaukee."

She laughed. "Well, I don't think this would be the same man. He sounded quite young to me."

"No, that first Mr. Lawdry that I met was almost a hundred years old. It will be interesting to meet another Lawdry though. "

"And now you're almost a hundred years old, Patrick."

There was a twinkle in his eye. "Perhaps, I will be the one who can do a favor for a Lawdry now in my old age."

Chapter Two

An hour went by. The wind grew stronger. Patrick Smithson sat staring out at the cold white world of swirling snow. He could barely see the shed where the caretaker kept his tools. The three Colorado Blue spruce along the entrance to the building swayed from one side to the other as if dancing to some inner silent rhythm. Patrick knew that if the spruce trees were moving like that, the wind must be strong. Would his guest arrive in this weather? Perhaps tomorrow.

After two hours of looking out the window and waiting, Patrick had given up. He didn't blame the person

18

at all. Nothing was important enough to risk your life driving in these conditions. He had settled down in his chair and started working on a crossword puzzle, when the door opened and Karen stood just inside the room with a big smile on her face. She gushed whenever someone came for a visit. Patrick had been here long enough to witness it many times over. Not that she was a bad person; this was only her job. When she went home, he knew she never thought about the people forced to live here. He also surmised that she had her own problems to deal with there.

A man with straight black hair that touched his shoulders and deep blue eyes, which were not a common combination, emerged from behind her. Patrick thought he must be well over six feet tall. Yes, he knew the Lawdry men were tall. Even bent with old age, Winnipesaukee had stood above him.

"Come in," he said, placing the crossword puzzle on the small table and smiling a welcome. "You must be the Mr. Lawdry who was coming to visit. I wouldn't have blamed you a bit if you'd stayed home in this nasty weather. That's a vicious storm out there." He motioned for the man to come closer. "Excuse me if I don't get up. I went for a rather long walk this morning and my legs don't seem to want to hold me up after that."

The stranger walked over and shook Patrick's hand. It was a firm handshake and Patrick marveled at the strength in it. Meanwhile, Karen fussed over the pillows on his bed before finally getting one of his chairs and moving it over for the man to sit on. The room was small but there was enough room for Patrick and the visitor to sit facing each other in front of the window.

With a flustered look and a wave of her arm, Karen apologized for the mess. There was no mess at all and she had never worried about how his room looked before. After several seconds of uncomfortable silence, she asked if they might like a cup of coffee. The man looked at Patrick. "That would be very nice. Would you like one, Mr. Smithson?"

"I think that would be wonderful, young man," he said turning to Karen with a smile.

Karen's cheeks were a bit pinker than normal and for a second Patrick wondered if she wasn't feeling well. However, on now seeing this Mr. Lawdry up close, he realized why. His visitor was an extremely comely looking man. What his exact age was, it was hard to say. Although he had noticed the blue eyes and dark hair, he hadn't realized what a deep penetrating blue those eyes were, how white and straight his teeth were, or that the structure of his face reminded him of a finely carved sculpture. He was also a well-dressed man, wearing a long dark woolen coat with a white silk scarf around his neck and holding black leather gloves in his hands. His hands, Patrick noticed, were not calloused and there was no dirt under his fingernails. The old man took all of this in at a glance.

"Yes, that would be nice. It's not often I have an extra cup of coffee in the afternoon." He spoke to his guest first and then turning to Karen, he said, with a wink, "Perhaps, we can make this a regular habit."

"Perhaps," she mumbled through her teeth but somehow managing to smile at the stranger at the same time. "I'll pop into the kitchen and see if someone can bring out a fresh pot."

When she had left the room, Patrick said, "Of course, you realize that I'll never have another treat like this again."

The stranger laughed. "Unless we have many more visits, perhaps?" His eyes smiled and his laugh was gentle.

"I like you already and I have no idea who you are. I thought Mrs. Freeman said you were a Lawdry?"

The visitor nodded. "That's right, and I've come a long way to meet you, Mr. Smithson. You probably don't know it but you are somewhat of a legend to me. My mother and I were not sure if you really existed so I decided to spend some time to search for you."

Patrick laughed. He was surprised how comfortable he could feel in this man's presence.

"It's a good thing you started now because soon I will be only a legend. I'm not getting younger and that's a fact. What did you hear about me that it was so important for you to meet me?"

"For one thing, we know someone named Patrick Smithson met a Frank Lawdry many years ago."

Patrick slowly nodded. It had been many years since he'd heard anyone use the name Frank Lawdry.

"And which Lawdry am I speaking to now? I'm sorry that I haven't even asked your first name, sir."

"My name is Michael Lawdry. Again, I'm not sure but I believe you might have known my father, Tobias."

Patrick stared at the man. "You are Toby's son? That little boy, Toby?"

Michael Lawdry laughed and nodded. "Yes. Even when I was a small boy, I still remember my father talking about you. Sometimes it seemed that you were someone he had made up in his imagination."

Patrick laughed. "Oh no, I was very real ... as was your father. Where is your father now? You must bring him to see me."

"My father died quite some time ago. When I was about six, he was killed in an accident."

"I am so sorry. What sort of accident?"

"We were living in a small town in Montana and my father served on the police force there. Unfortunately, there was a chase and my father's car flipped over. They said he was killed instantly."

The old man smiled. "So he really did become an officer of the law. He told me that he wanted to join the RCMP when he grew up. I guess he did the next best thing. I'm proud of him."

The door opened and Karen swept in with a tray filled with ham and cheese sandwiches, store bought cookies, and steaming coffee. By the time she had arranged the tray on a small table, fixed their coffee for them, and stood lingering, asking if there was more she could do, Patrick was getting impatient with her.

22

"That's all, Mrs. Freeman," he said, "You may go now. If we need anything more, we'll shout."

Patrick knew he might pay for it later but it was worth it just to see the look on Karen's face. How many times did he have to remind her that she worked for him and not the other way around? He turned back to Michael.

With a twinkle in his eye, he said, "You know if I ever did shout for her, I would be thrown out into a snow bank." They laughed together. Patrick pointed to the coffee and the food. "Please, Michael, help yourself."

In between sipping coffee and eating, they talked.

"You know, Michael, when you say I met Frank Lawdry, I have to stop and think, because the man I met didn't call himself Frank Lawdry. He used the name Winnipesaukee. If I remember correctly, it was the name given to him by an Abenaki Indian tribe. Did you know that?"

"Winnipesaukee?" He smiled and nodded. "Yes, I knew that was Frank Lawdry's Indian name but no one has spoken it for many years now."

The old man took a few moments to dunk his cookie into the coffee and take a bite.

"But, of course, at that time, I had no idea he was Frank Lawdry. I was a young man back then, away from home for the first time, and Winnipesaukee was about a hundred years old." Patrick leaned back in his chair and reminisced. That was so long ago. "He was quite the old fellow." He laughed. "He kept me up all night, telling me the story of your family."

23

His visitor looked up from his cup. "Do you remember any of it?"

Patrick gazed out at the flakes coming down. There were less now and the wind had died down.

"I can recall some but I'm afraid most of it has left my mind. As a young man sent out into the unknown world, you tend to think more of your own circumstances than remember the story of someone else's. And my own life took many twists and turns during that period of time."

"Yes, I suppose your own situation would take priority over an old man's history. What about my father? Do you know anything about him?"

Patrick picked up the carafe and refilled their cups. Usually his hands shook but for some reason, he felt strong and young again. He felt better reliving the past than living in the present.

"I only knew your father when he was a small boy. I suppose he was like any other youngster in some ways but in other ways, he was one of a kind." He paused. "Yes, Toby Lawdry was a unique little boy."

"Really? I always thought of him as being an exceptional individual too but perhaps all children think that way about their fathers." He stopped to pour cream into his coffee and stir it. "When did you meet him? I don't understand that part. It seems as if there's an empty page in my family history. You spoke of Winnipesaukee but I know nothing about him."

"Did you know he had a sister named Sarah?"

Michael said nothing for several moments as he held his cup with both hands, and stared outside. He slowly turned and looked at Patrick. "Sarah? Yes, come to think of it, I did see that name. I found an old photo in a box. It was a picture of three people. Someone wrote their names on it - Sarah, Frank, and a man named Louis. I had no idea who Sarah was. So that was Winnipesaukee and his sister, Sarah?"

Patrick's face lit up and he nodded. "Yes, I saw that picture once too. Well, actually twice, you could say. The second time, I hid it. Toby must have gone back and found it before the fire. The first time I saw it, it was on the wall in the old cabin where Winnipesaukee lived. Sarah lived there first by herself until Frank came back to her. The Louis in the photo was Louis Riel."

His visitor stared at him. "That was Louis Riel, the leader of the Métis?"

Patrick nodded. "Oh yes, they were turbulent times when your relatives lived in the Qu'Appelle Valley. Did you know that Winnipesaukee called the valley, Sarah's Valley?"

Michael shook his head. "Why would he do that?"

"Oh, it is such a long story. I did have some of it written down once but sadly, it was destroyed and I didn't have the heart at the time to rewrite it." Patrick was now feeling the effects of his long morning walk.

Perhaps, Michael Lawdry noticed because he said, "Could I come back? I'm staying in the hotel not far from here. I'm off work for the next two weeks. Can you tell me a little every day until I get the whole story? I don't want to tire you out."

Patrick nodded and smiled. "I am not as strong as Winnipesaukee. He told his story in one night and he was older than I am now. No, my friend, come tomorrow and as many days after as it takes, and I will tell you all that I remember. Perhaps the more I talk about it, the more memories will return. As you can see, I'm not going anywhere. I wish I could recall all that Frank Lawdry told me but I'm sorry that I cannot. I can, however, tell you about your father, Toby, and how he started out as a young boy." He stopped and chuckled. "Yes, your father and I had some adventures of our own."

Michael grinned. "That is why I came. I want to learn my heritage. I want to know about my father. He's been a mystery for too long."

"Well, I will do my best to fill in the empty spaces. But, tell me, how did you find out about me? Was it because your father spoke of me often?"

The visitor nodded. "He mentioned your name many times, but as a child, I must admit I didn't think too much about it. As I said, you were more like a mythical character. That is, until I found your name on a piece of paper. Then it struck me that this was the person my father talked about so much."

"You found my name on a piece of paper?"

"Yes. It was very old and tattered, and stuck in the back of that picture frame. Just from reading the note, I thought you must be the one my father spoke about." He

26

reached into his pocket, brought out his wallet, and removed a piece of yellowed paper. He handed it to Patrick.

As soon as he saw it, Patrick knew what it said. He could not believe that he was holding a note that he had written eighty years before. Tears came to his eyes.

That old man, who looked like Moses to a young Patrick Smithson, had kept the piece of paper where Patrick had written: Thank you for the food and the story, Mr. Winnipesaukee, but I must leave now and go to my new job. If my car won't start, I will walk to the highway and catch the bus. I hope I will see you again someday. Sincerely yours, Patrick Smithson.

"So did you ever see Frank Lawdry again?"

Patrick could not stop the tears from running down his cheeks. What memories this brought back. He quickly wiped them away with his hand.

"I'm sorry, Mr. Smithson. Is this going to be too difficult for you? I don't want you to be upset."

Patrick shook his head. "No, I wouldn't call it difficult - perhaps, overwhelming might be a better word to describe my emotions."

"So you will be up to telling me about my father?"

"Oh yes, however, it will have to wait until the morning. I'm afraid I've tuckered myself out for this day."

The younger man smiled and Patrick couldn't help but remember the blue eyes of that little boy named Toby Lawdry.

"In fact, Michael Lawdry," he said," I will try to tell you my story as well, just as your ancestor told his to me."

27

Mr. Lawdry stood and bent down to shake Patrick's hand.

"I would like that very much."

Chapter Three

*A*lthough he'd spent a listless night, tossing and turning in his bed, Patrick woke up with a spring in his step. In his mind, he kept going over events from the past. If only he still had the story he'd written after he left Fort Qu'Appelle. It had taken all winter to write but it helped get through those cold evenings, and Molly ... well, Molly loved listening to that story. If only his father-in-law hadn't burned their cabin down before he could remove all of his belongings. At the time, he hadn't even thought about the notepad that his wife had kept in the top drawer of the bureau in the bedroom. All he thought about was leaving before Jacob Jordan shot a hole in his heart.

When Karen came in to work the next morning, she made a beeline for Patrick's room. Breakfast was over and Patrick sat by the window, staring out at nothing, with a notebook and pen in hand. He had tried to write something down but his mind was blank. Why couldn't he remember?

At one time, those days spent with Toby and Winnipesaukee had meant so much to him. Did he think because he wouldn't have that many years left that there was no need to remember? Now he had more reason than ever to remember and keep living. His life wasn't over yet; he had a story to tell. He couldn't help feeling excited at the thought.

"Patrick Smithson," Karen said, standing at the door with her hands on her hips, "I don't think it was very appropriate for you to be ordering me about as you did yesterday. I was kind to you because you had company but today is another day so don't expect any special treatment. Things are back to normal. Do you understand?"

Patrick gazed out the window. The sun was shining, turning the snow banks into mounds of sparkling silver. It was a deceiving sight, however, as Patrick knew the sun did not send any heat down with its rays. He watched as the caretaker, Tom Hillard, cleared off the walkway. Even from inside and the furnace sending heat up through the vents, he could still hear the snow crunching under his feet and could see Tom's breath frozen in the air. He hoped Michael Lawdry would come soon.

"Patrick, I know you can hear me. I said that you are not to expect any special treatment today. I did you a favor because you had company. The next time someone comes to visit, maybe we can do it again. Understood?"

Patrick turned to her. "Karen, I am ninety-five years old; however, I am not dead yet. Or, deaf for that matter. I don't even have to wear glasses every day as you do. It wouldn't kill you to bring out a cup of coffee in the afternoon for those who might like it. Not everyone would want one and some days, I might even refuse. It would be very kind of you to do that though."

Karen cleared her throat. "You don't seem to grasp the concept of a budget, do you? I have to watch every penny I spend in this place. Maybe before we spend money for coffee, we might consider using the money for more necessary things."

"Like?"

"Well, I can't think of something offhand; however, I do know there are more pressing issues than people having an afternoon coffee break."

Her name sounded over the loudspeaker and she turned to go.

"Saved by the bell, Karen," Patrick said. "Let me know when you can come up with an answer."

The director gave him a withering look and turned to leave. Before she had taken a step, Michael Lawdry stood in front of her, blocking her way.

"Oh, Mr. Lawdry," she gasped. "I didn't even hear you coming down the hallway." Patrick watched as a deep pink spread from somewhere beneath her shirt and up through her face.

Michael grinned and Patrick wondered if the man even knew what affect he had on women. With a slight bow, he handed Karen the envelope he had been holding in his hand.

She stood mesmerized as he handed her the envelope.

31

"This is for me?" she managed to blurt out.

Michael nodded. "It is. This will help cover any expenses that Patrick and I might incur during the next few days." He turned to Patrick and winked. "We don't want to be a burden on the Home here, right, Patrick?"

"Right, Mr. Lawdry." He tried to keep a serious look but couldn't stop the grin from spreading across his face.

With a flushed face, Karen replied, "Oh, Mr. Lawdry, that isn't necessary. Really, I don't mind you and Patrick having a cup of coffee in his room." She tucked the envelope into her pocket. "In fact," she said with a laugh, "I'll notify the kitchen and if I can, I'll bring it to you myself when it's ready." And with that, she disappeared down the hallway.

"That's a good one," Patrick said. "Now she's committed. How many cups of coffee did you pay for anyway?"

Michael laughed and pulled up his chair to face the old man. "About four hundred."

Patrick must have looked shocked because Michael reached over and patted his shoulder. "Don't worry; we can spend as much time as we want together. For the money that's left over, I'll make sure you get an afternoon coffee break for many days to come."

Already Patrick could discern that this Lawdry had inherited many of the same qualities as his precursors. He could imagine Winnipesaukee or Toby handling the situation exactly the same way.

One of the aides brought the coffee along with cookies about fifteen minutes later. She was one of the older workers and Patrick loved listening to her lilting English accent. It brought back memories of his own mother who, even after many years in Canada, had never lost her London accent.

"So nice to see you've got some company, Patrick," she said as she poured the coffee. "And I'll put the carafe over on the table here in case you want more later. If it's cold, you give me a shout, luv."

"Margaret, this here is Michael Lawdry. He's come to hear about some of his relatives that I knew many years ago."

Margaret's face softened. "Ah, that's wonderful. So many nowadays don't care about anything from the past. Where are you from, Mr. Lawdry?"

Patrick felt his face redden. That was a question he hadn't even asked.

Michael smiled. "I'm from down east, ma'am. From a little place called New York City."

Margaret stared for a moment and burst out laughing. "Oh, you had me there for a second. Well, you'll find this little town to be pretty boring."

He glanced outside. The day was clear and with the bare branches on the trees, a person could see far across the prairie. The seniors' Home was on the outskirts of town so there were no homes or businesses blocking the view. To Patrick, this wasn't much of a view unless you enjoyed looking out at nothing.

"This is a rare treat, Margaret. Where I live, I see only concrete and brick. I can only imagine looking out and seeing such a peaceful scene as this."

She nodded. "I suppose it's all in the eye of the beholder. Well, I best get on with my work. Mrs. Freeman seems to be biting at the bit today." She rolled her eyes at Patrick. "If you know what I mean."

Margaret left and gently shut the door. The two men sat in a comfortable silence as they each dunked their cookies and drank their coffee.

"I didn't realize you'd come so far to see me," Patrick said. "This must be very important to you."

Michael thought for a moment. "I guess you could say that. My life has too many unanswered questions. I need to fill them in."

"Where's your mother, Michael? Was she left to raise you on your own after Toby died?"

"My mother remarried not long after my father died. She has since passed away. He was a wealthy man who was good to us. I can't complain except that he wasn't a real father. I believe I was considered something like perhaps an extra suitcase that happened to come with my mother. However, he made sure I was fed and cared for."

"Sort of like a family pet?"

He laughed. "Sort of."

"By the looks of you, he must have cared for you pretty good."

"He did see to it that I went to the best schools and that I received a good education."

"So what is it you do, Michael?"

"I'm a professor at one of the private colleges in New York City."

"Really? I was a teacher too." He laughed. "Not quite at a professor's level though. Tell me, what made you pick that career?"

Michael shook his head. "I know this sounds strange but it was actually my father who put that thought into my head."

"Did he tell you that you would be good at teaching boys?"

"Why, yes he did. How did you know?"

Patrick chuckled. "Just a wild guess."

Michael refilled their cups.

"What happened after your mother died, Michael? Do you keep in touch with your stepfather?"

"I guess the sad part was that when my mother died, he and I went our separate ways. I really didn't mind as I was busy making my own life but I felt sorry for him."

"Where is he?"

"He's in a nursing home in upstate New York. His money will look after him until he dies but he has dementia so bad he doesn't know where he is or who he is anymore."

"Do you go to visit him at all?"

Michael shrugged. "I did a few times when he was first admitted but now he doesn't recognize me at all. No, the money I have, I have worked for myself, Patrick. I really have no need for all the money I will be inheriting. In fact, I'm not sure what I'll even do with it."

Patrick nodded. "You are a good man, Michael Lawdry. It was never an easy life for me but I have always been able to hold my head high too."

"Why don't you tell me your story now, Patrick?"

"Yes, well, if I'm going to, I suppose I should get started." He paused and stared at the white world outside. With a sad smile, he said, "It's too bad we aren't sitting outside in front of a fire now, isn't it? That's where the best stories are told."

Michael laughed. "Is that where you heard the story from Winnipesaukee?"

"Yes, it is. In fact, it was a perfect spot for storytelling. The fire burned high, the river flowed gently by, the loons called not far away, and our bellies were full."

"It sounds like you could have been there yesterday. Do you remember what your bellies were full of?"

Patrick grinned. "Mostly I remember the potatoes fried in bacon grease. Whatever it was, to a young lad who was half starving, it was the best meal in the world."

Both men were silent for a few moments. Perhaps each was imagining himself back there by the river, sitting outside of Winnipesaukee's small cabin. In the air was the mixed smell of wood burning, bacon frying, and coffee boiling. Patrick would never forget the taste of that strong coffee. He'd never tasted anything like it before and for sure, never again.

The younger man smiled at the old one. "I don't care how you tell it, Patrick, just tell me the story as best you *remember. I will always appreciate the time you are taking for me."*

Tears welled up in the storyteller's eyes. Yes, he thought, there is such a story to tell.

Chapter Four

I'll always remember waking up that morning in Sarah's valley...We'd been up most of the night. I don't know when Mr. Winnipesaukee slept. The sun was so hot on my face that morning. I jumped up and looked around, wondering where I was. The campfire was out and when I called, no one answered. I still remember that the only sounds I heard were the rustling of leaves, the gentle slap of water on the shore, and a call from a loon far down the river.

Sitting on a large rock, I listened for quite some time to the slow moving water. I felt so alone in the world. Even when I tried whistling a tune, it sounded empty as if the breeze had stolen the song from my lips. I don't know why but there was something about that river that made me melancholy. In front of the cabin, it wasn't very wide and it looked quite brown if I remember correctly. Winnipesaukee said it sometimes flooded its banks but that year it was low. It was during what everyone called 'the Dirty Thirties.' The land was desiccated and grasshoppers were the only ones eating the crops ... if there were any crops. We could see where the grasshoppers marched across the land, leaving a line of total devastation. Those were the most devastating ten years on record.

Most fields stood bare with only short stocks of wheat or barley standing. Sometimes we would have dust storms and even inside the house, we'd have to cover our faces with rags because that dust seeped in through every miniscule opening. For the farmers who managed to sow some kind of crop, the wind came up and swept all the topsoil along with the seeds away. Sometimes the only vegetation we saw was the tumbleweeds blowing and bouncing across the dead prairie land. No one back then had ever seen anything like it and I've never seen anything like it again.

My pa and grandpa lived in northern Saskatchewan. In some ways, it was better than the south because there was bush and bluffs of trees but the land itself was bone dry. They had decided to homestead there because the government was selling land cheap. Now, however, they had no way of making a living, as they only knew working the land. Both my grandma and my ma had died and were buried a ways back from the house. A little brother of mine was buried there too. I will always remember how I missed my mother. She was a lovely soul and didn't belong up in the bush, working so hard all day long. I'm sure it was that hard work that killed her. I believe Pa thought so too although he never said it.

The land barely supplied enough food for us to eat. The few cows we had were not in very good shape and didn't give much milk anymore. So, Pa and Grandpa decided that I should leave the farm and find a job, working on someone else's land. I was doing no one any good wasting my time on a dying farm.

There was an ad in the newspaper. Well, it wasn't a newspaper like we have today. I think it was called *The Producer* or something like that. Anyway, it was mostly for farming folks. The ad I answered was asking for a farmer's helper down in Saskatchewan somewhere south between Moose Jaw and Swift Current. The description said it must be a strong healthy young man, able to drive a tractor, a team of horses, and have some knowledge of a threshing machine just in case there might be a crop to thresh some day. You had to have that kind of humor in those days. I applied and lo and behold, I got the job. Perhaps, I was the only one who applied. This was the late thirties and there was talk of war in Europe during those years so many young fellows were joining the army, many because it would mean a job with food to eat and a place to sleep. The thought of actually being called up and going across the ocean to fight didn't enter their minds. I didn't have a hankering for joining the army. If it did happen that Canada had to join in the fight, I didn't want to be guilty of taking someone's life, even if he was an enemy. I couldn't stomach the thought of that.

My pa traded me the little mare I had for his old Model T Ford. Or, maybe it was a Model A. Whatever it was, it was old but in those days, you could fix almost anything - car, truck, tractor - with a piece of binder twine. It purred along without a hitch but when I got down into the Qu'Appelle Valley, it conked out, and I was wishing I'd taken my little horse. Pa thought I would look more qualified for the job if I drove a car into the yard instead of riding in on a tired horse. Besides, they'd loaded me up with so many jars of food, I didn't have much choice.

When the car decided to call it quits and putter to a stop, I thought for sure I would never reach my destination. I would lose that job and probably have to hitch a ride all the way back up north. Mechanics had never been my strong suit no matter how much my grandfather tried to teach me. My father wasn't much better at it than I was.

I jumped out of the car and was trying to figure out why it wouldn't start, when I looked up and saw Winnipesaukee. He appeared out of nowhere. Even for being so old and bent, he was still taller than I was. He had long white hair and a long beard that reached to his waist. His face had more wrinkles than I could count. What a picture he made!

Well, that old man caught me saying a few choice words to that vehicle. Yes sir, he sort of sprang out of nowhere and scared the life out of me. He invited me to his place so I went, following behind him through the dust stirred up by his moccasins, to his cabin. What excuse could I make for not going? I certainly had nowhere else to go.

I have to admit that I'm glad I followed that old fellow. He cooked me up some good vittles and got the fire roaring. I didn't know it then but it was a night that would mold my life forever.

I remember telling him that while a person's sitting by the fire, someone should tell a story. A young man of sixteen doesn't have much of a story to tell but that old man could weave a tale, let me tell you. He took me back to the very start of Sarah's and his journey across America. Of course, as he's telling it I have no idea he's the young man in the story. In fact, he went back even further, telling me all about his ancestors. I didn't care much for history in school but Winnipesaukee made it all come alive to me. A few years later, I wrote it down in a big notebook but sadly, I don't have that anymore.

"What happened to it?" Michael asked. "You said it got burned?"

Patrick nodded. "Yes. That, along with many more memories."

"How did that happen?"

Patrick shook his head. "That's where Winnipesaukee's story stops and mine begins."

"What do you mean, Patrick?"

"Well, if you've the time for it, I'll tell you my tale. It has a connection to the Lawdry family too."

"You mean my father?"

The old man nodded. "Yes, indeed. The Lawdry family has made quite an impact on my life."

Michael smiled. "I have all the time in the world."

I worked for a Mr. Jacob Jordan. He was farming a section and a half of barren land. Most of it was sown in grain but he had some livestock too. As soon as I set eyes on him, I could see that he wasn't a healthy man but he seemed to function on an abundance of nervous energy. He wasn't the type of man a person could get close to or feel particularly relaxed with. When he spoke to you, which was mostly to give orders, he never quite looked you in the eye. Later, neighbors told me a few farmhands had tried working for the man but they walked away or Mr. Jordan ordered them to walk away. It was a large farm though, as all farms in Saskatchewan were, and he worked it alone. Mr. and Mrs. Jordan had no sons and only one daughter. Her name was Molly.

I will always remember the day I drove up in that old car with smoke pouring out from under the hood. My fan belt had come off about a mile from the farm and I figured I could make it to my destination without the engine seizing up. That was my grand entrance. Jacob Jordan didn't look too impressed. Mrs. Jordan looked relieved that I'd arrived and Molly stood by the door with a sweet smile on her lips.

"Well, young man," Mr. Jordan said. "I trust you'll look after my machinery better than you do your own."

"Yes, sir," I said. "I usually do look after my own real good too but I knew I was a day late and I wanted to get here as fast as I could."

Mr. Jordan grunted, pointed to the bunkhouse, and said, "Get yourself settled in there and come in for supper at six. You'll be eating your breakfast with us at five-thirty every morning except Sunday. My wife will give you some sandwiches for your noon meal that you can eat as you work. Sunday is the Lord's Day here so it'd be good for you to save up some of your Saturday food. You have Sunday for your own. I won't tolerate coming in late Saturday night after an evening of drinking though. You do that and you'll be on your way. You understand, young man?"

I nodded. "Yes sir, Mr. Jordan."

After the first week, I was about to walk off but I knew my pa would be disappointed. I had to stay until I had some money saved up.

By the second week, I still hated my job but how I looked forward to seeing Molly at suppertime every day. Jacob and I sat all by ourselves at the large kitchen table while his wife and daughter brought us our food. I must admit, they didn't skimp on the food. It was almost worth the abuse I took every day from Mr. Jordan. But seeing Molly's smile was worth more than all that money could buy. We dared not speak to each other at mealtime but our eyes would meet and that said it all.

One morning, after I'd been there for about a month, I heard the barn door slide open. I'd always loved horses and Mr. Jordan didn't seem too interested in any of them so I tried to spend a bit of time pampering them when I could. If he'd caught me giving the little mare a rubdown, he would surely have sent me out to chop wood, or do anything but waste time brushing a horse. I quickly put the brush down and picked up the pitchfork. If a man is busy working, he doesn't stop to listen to any noise so I kept pitching hay, hoping my boss would see me working and leave. I didn't hear anything more so I stopped and looked up. There stood Molly watching me with shining eyes and a smile on her lips.

"What are you doing out in the barn? This is no place for a lady like you." I asked. My heart was beating so fast, I moved the pitchfork in front of me in case she could see my shirt pounding.

She laughed. "Why do you think, Patrick?"

"You came out to milk the cow?"

I still remember her laughter. After that little encounter, we made secret plans to meet almost every day. It was a special treat if we found a few minutes alone out in the woods. In those days, a stolen kiss was something special.

Molly was the prettiest girl I'd ever seen. Not that I'd seen many young women but I did look at a few in magazines whenever I had the chance. Her hair was a soft blond color and her eyes were light blue. She was quite a bit shorter than I was so her head nestled perfectly against me as we sat in the tall grass and planned our life together. It did not cross our minds that we were still teenagers.

There was a bluff of trees about a mile from the house so she would arrange to walk to the neighbor's, about three miles away, and I would happen to ride out into the far pasture to check on the fences. Molly's parents didn't suspect a thing. However, before the summer was over, we knew we had to be together forever. We couldn't meet secretly any longer and yet we knew her parents would not approve of our relationship.

One morning, while Mr. Jordan and I were having our breakfast, Molly entered the room. I was quite taken aback too as she was never up this early. I stopped eating and stared at her.

"What is it, girl?" Mr. Jordan asked.

Molly smiled and came over and stood behind me. She put her arm around my shoulder and stood very close.

I watched as her father's eyes widened and filled with rage.

"Molly," he said, in a low seething voice, "Remove your arm from around that young man right now."

Molly shook her head. I could not come to her rescue. My tongue lay paralyzed in my mouth.

"Father, you might as well know that Patrick and I are planning to marry." She put her head down and softly kissed my cheek. All I could do was keep my eyes on her father. He stood up very slowly. His face was now a deep scarlet. He clenched the back of his chair so hard I could see his knuckles turning white.

At that moment, Mrs. Jordan walked into the room, carrying the large coffee pot. Her eyes widened when she saw Molly with her arm around me. She glanced over and when she saw the look on her husband's face, she dropped the coffee pot. The thud of the pot hitting the floor sounded like a bomb going off and the boiling hot coffee sprayed up in all directions.

For the next several minutes, Mr. Jordan took turns yelling at his wife and yelling at Molly but the brunt of his anger was towards me.

"I gave you a job and this is what you do to me? You spend your time seducing my little girl?" He shook his fist so close to my face, I could smell the bacon grease on his hand. "You pack up your things and get out of here. If I see your face again, I won't ask questions. I'll shoot you. You got that, Mr. Smithson?"

"No, papa, no," Molly was screaming. "I love him. We love each other. If you hurt Patrick, I'll leave and never come back."

Meanwhile, Mrs. Jordan had her apron up to her face, crying into it as if her world had come to an end.

Eventually, everyone calmed down. All the while, I had not said a word.

Mr. Jordan's color returned to normal and Mrs. Jordan's wailing ceased. Molly sobbed quietly but never left my side.

"Mr. Jordan," I said, "Molly and I never planned on this happening. We just grew very fond of each other. I would never take advantage of her. I care too much for her. And she's right; we do want to spend the rest of our lives together."

Molly's parents took turns trying to reason with us. They started out calmly but when they saw we would not change our minds, Mr. Jordan returned to the threats and Mrs. Jordan returned to sobbing and beating her hands on her chest.

In the end, Mr. Jordan said he was going into town to the bank and would give me my pay for the month plus some extra, even though the month wasn't finished.

"You take this money, Patrick, and go back to your Pa. We don't need the likes of you around here. Maybe come back in a couple of years and see if you and Molly still care for each other. I'm doing you a big favor, boy."

"I don't want your money, sir, I want your daughter." I might not have been so brave but I felt Molly's hand on my shoulder and I felt that I could do anything.

Mr. Jordan's body started to shake with rage.

"You get out of my house and off my land. I want you gone by the morning. You got that, Smithson?"

Before I could say a word in my defense, he yanked me off the chair and physically threw me out the door. I tripped on the wooden steps and landed in a heap on the ground. Before I could get up, the door slammed shut, and I sat there wondering what I would do next. Slowly, I stood up, dusted myself off, and went to the bunkhouse.

As soon as it was dark, I snuck back to the house and tapped three times on Molly's bedroom window; then, I went back to the bunkhouse to wait.

At three a.m., we met in the bluff of trees north of the house. The moon was high and there was a chill in the air. We had a long trek across fields and pastures before we reached the main road. I carried a gunnysack with a few essentials and Molly clutched a small suitcase. We had prepared for this, days in advance. No matter what the outcome with her parents, whether we received their blessing or we didn't, we were going to be together for the rest of our lives.

It was almost morning before a farmer hauling a load of grain gave us a ride as far as Gravelbourg. If he was suspicious, he didn't let on and he never asked any questions. He was probably more concerned about the sale of his grain and wondering if the bit of money he would receive would keep him and his family alive for the winter.

He stopped the truck on the outskirts of town.

"Well, here you are," he said. "From here, I head to the elevator. I hope you find your folks all right. Don't worry; the Lord will take care of you." He smiled down at us, waved, and drove off.

"He thought we were orphans looking for our parents," I said to Molly.

She smiled. "We do look like lost souls, don't we? Maybe we should go and have some breakfast. I have enough money for that."

I grabbed her hand and we walked the last mile into town. We entered the first restaurant we found and had a hearty breakfast, which was good because that had to last us for quite some time. However, we still needed a ride to Swift Current. We had to get as far away from her parents as we could.

It didn't take long for someone to pick us up along the highway. This time it was a travelling salesman and he was aching to have someone to talk to. The rest of the drive went by quickly.

Our next hurdle was finding someone to marry us. Our first stop was the Courthouse and from there, they sent us to a private home. It was a small white house with red trim and a wide veranda. By the front door, there was a small sign that said, 'Justice of the Peace.'

"You're wanting to marry, are you?" The older man who answered our knock was short, stocky, and bald except for a ring of white hair that grew from above his ears, around the back of his head, and back up to the other ear. His glasses sat on the tip of his nose. The lenses were so thick, that when he pushed his glasses up, his eyes looked about four times their size.

He looked at us again and I knew he was probably almost blind.

"Sir," I said. "I'm eighteen and my future wife is seventeen." In reality, I was almost seventeen and Molly was fifteen.

If his eyesight had been 20/20, he might have questioned that information.

"All right," he said. "Give me the $2.00 first."

I handed him the two one-dollar bills. He squinted as he held them up about an inch from his face.

He nodded and held the inside door open for us.

"Where are your witnesses?" he asked.

Molly and I looked at each other. We didn't know we had to have witnesses.

"Never mind," he said, "I'll get my wife. She and I can be your witnesses."

"Thank you," I said.

"That will be another seventy-five cents," he said, and held out his hand.

Getting hitched cost more than what we'd expected.

It wasn't fancy and it wasn't romantic. I didn't even get to kiss the bride, but after we'd signed the papers and walked out, we felt like we were walking on clouds.

"Well, Mrs. Smithson," I said, "Where should we spend the night?"

Molly giggled. "Somewhere where my parents won't find us," she said, and we laughed and kissed right there on the street. We were husband and wife and nothing could separate us now.

"Look," Molly said, as we walked down to the main street, "There's a hotel on the corner. The Imperial Hotel. Let's go and see if we can get a room."

I checked to see how much money we had. Counting all our change, we had one dollar and thirty-two cents left.

"If we can get a room for one dollar," I said, "we will have enough for a thirty cent breakfast."

It turned out that for one dollar, we could get a small room at the back of the hotel, looking out onto the back alley, and for breakfast, we could have all the coffee and toast that we could eat.

"You're sure you're married?" the man at the desk asked. "We are a respectable hotel and we don't want angry parents showing up in the night to take you home."

I handed him our marriage certificate.

He grinned. "This is today's date on here. This is your wedding day?"

We both nodded.

"Well, I'm sure we can find something to make this day special for you." He took the key back from me and handed me another one. "This one is better for newlyweds."

We walked up the stairs to the top floor and unlocked the door of our hotel room. Both of us stood and gazed in amazement. Neither one of us had ever seen such a beautiful room. Not only did we have a large bed with a fancy bedcover, we had our own private bathroom with a big soaker tub.

"My parents will never find us here," Molly said, laughing. With that, we shut and locked the door, and had the most wonderful wedding night that any couple could have ever had.

The next morning, we showed up for breakfast, looking a bit flushed but sparkling clean after soaking together in that big bathtub. I'm sure most of the staff and the other patrons were watching us but we couldn't take our eyes off each other. Not only did we get the toast and coffee, we dined on ham, eggs, and pancakes. It's hard to imagine enjoying a meal, not knowing when or where your next one will be, but when you're so much in love, you truly live for the moment.

When we got up to leave, everyone in the room clapped and wished us well. Molly took her box camera out of her valise and an older man who had been sitting beside us told us that if we went outside in the sunlight he would be pleased to take our picture. It was the most wonderful day of my life.

We were still glowing when we walked away from the hotel and down the sidewalk. The glow soon vanished when a police car drove up and stopped beside us. The driver rolled down his window.

"Patrick Smithson and Molly Jordan?"

"No," I said. "We're Mr. and Mrs. Smithson. Why do you want to know?"

"I've been dispatched to take Miss Jordan back to her parents and you Mr. Smithson, I will be escorting to jail." He opened the car door and got out.

"No," Molly said, holding onto my arm, "Patrick is my husband. We have our marriage license with us." She rummaged in her valise, pulled out the paper, and handed it to the man.

He skimmed over it and handed it back.

"Well," he said, "I better take you both back to your parents then, Mrs. Smithson. Since you're now legally married, I'll let you and your parents settle this between yourselves."

With a great deal of apprehension, we climbed into the back seat. There were a few curious onlookers gawking from the sidewalk but we both knew this was nothing compared to what would be awaiting us back at the farm. We sat close to each other and held hands. This day had to come and we couldn't wait to get it over with.

It was late in the afternoon when we finally drove into the farmyard. The driver, who was newly married himself, took pity on us and stopped along the way to buy us our dinner. It was a good meal but both our stomachs were in knots, worrying about what awaited us.

When Jacob Jordan saw that the two of us were together in the back seat of the patrol car, he raced back into the house and came out, carrying his shotgun. I don't know if he planned on shooting me in front of a law officer but that was what the officer understood was happening and he wasn't too pleased. After ordering us to duck down, the officer took out his revolver, opened the car door, and stood behind it, his gun trained on Mr. Jordan.

"Drop it, sir, or I'll shoot," he shouted. Mr. Jordan's eyes bulged as he slowly lowered his rifle. His wife stood by the door with her hands on her heart and her eyes filled with terror.

With his gun trained on Jacob Jordan, the officer walked slowly to the steps. He reached down, never taking his eyes off the assailant, and picked up the shotgun.

"I'll be confiscating this, Mr. Jordan," he said. "Now, I suggest you listen to these young people. They have a valid marriage license. Maybe you don't like it but what's been done has been done. My father-in-law can't stand me either but it's just the way it is. Get used to it."

With that, he walked to the car, opened our door, and told us to get out. He gently placed the shotgun on the backseat after removing the shells, and drove away.

Jacob wasn't too pleased about losing his shotgun but I could have revealed to the officer that he had two more out in the barn. All it took was one shell!

Mrs. Jordan's eyes told me that she was just happy to see Molly again.

"Go to your mom, Molly," I told her. "I'll go to the bunkhouse so when you're ready, come there."

She didn't say anything, just looked at me.

"That's all you have to do." I smiled. For a moment, she hesitated but then gave me a quick hug and ran to her mother.

Her father stalked away to the barn, undoubtedly to retrieve his other rifles.

For the next month, Jacob Jordan did not speak to his daughter or to her husband. We worked separately but I made sure to do extra work. Finally, after almost two months, he agreed with his wife that we should have our own little cabin. His daughter should not have to live in a cold drafty bunkhouse. Although it was February, the days were not too cold so we started on the cabin. If I thought working together building his daughter's future home would bring us closer, I was mistaken.

We didn't realize that as he and I worked on the log cabin that a tiny human being had already formed and was growing inside Molly.

Chapter Five

Patrick stopped. He could feel tears wanting to burst out but he forced himself to continue. This was the first time he had ever relived his past like this. Reliving the death of his wife and child was like reopening an old wound and pouring salt into it.

"Are you sure you want to continue, Patrick?"

Patrick nodded. "Yes, you have to know because this is where you father enters the picture. Let me tell you about life after my Molly died."

Why did it seem that every time I visited Molly's gravesite at night, the wind blew harder than ever, making the old trees creak and groan? Why did the old hoot owl and the black crows gather on the barren branches, screeching? It was as if the world was mourning Molly's death too.

The moon hid behind the clouds so that my only light was the lantern I'd borrowed from Nathan Pike. Mr. Pike was my new boss and I was pleased that he had some sincere feelings for me.

"You know, Patrick," he said, "Jacob Jordan isn't a wicked man. It's just that he's heartbroken over losing his only daughter. He's hurting the same as you."

Nathan Pike never said anything very quickly. The most would be two sentences and then he'd have a puff on his pipe before speaking again.

"Now I can't pay you quite as much as he did but I can give you a roof over your head and my missus can fill your belly. Yes sir, and I can give you some pocket change every week or so." He tapped his pipe on his bottom teeth before puffing on it and blowing its bluish smoke into the air. I didn't mind Mr. Pike's pipe and found the sweet smell of that smoke quite relaxing. "I think you give him some time, he'll come round to treating you right. No sir, he ain't a bad man at heart."

"I don't mind that he doesn't want to have anything to do with me, sir; it's the shooting at me part that I'm not too keen on."

It was after dinner that we'd had this conversation. We were sitting in the living room. Mrs. Pike was in the kitchen cleaning up the dishes. Mary Pike didn't like me much because Molly's mother was her best friend. I'd heard her a few times telling her husband that she didn't want me there. For some reason, all the older women thought I'd seduced Molly because that's just what young men do.

"All they want is to get some nice young girl into bed with them," she had said. "They're all like a bunch of animals at that age."

All Mr. Pike did was keep puffing on his pipe.

"If it wasn't for that boy wanting to get that young girl in bed, she'd still be alive today."

Every time I heard that, my blood ran cold. But I never said a word because Mr. Pike said it the best.

After puffing several times, he answered, "Don't think that girl was forced into that bed. She went willingly just like you used to when you were her age."

Since neither one had seen or heard me come into the kitchen, I took my leave and scooted out to the barn before they caught me eavesdropping. After hearing that, I felt that I held a secret over Mrs. Pike and whenever she would give me an evil look, I'd give her a knowing look and a little smile. Every time I did, her face would turn pink and she would turn away. I believe her husband's words were coming back to her.

So every Saturday evening I would sneak out after dark and drive the five miles to the graveyard. I would sit and visit with Molly for about an hour and then head back home. I told Mr. Pike about it and he had no problem lending me the old farm truck. I didn't take any chances with Mrs. Pike hearing the motor so I would push the truck to the top of the hill, jump in, and coast to the bottom. That was a sure way of getting the old thing to start too.

One night when I was talking to Molly, I came upon a decision. Not that I believed she could hear me. I knew she was lying dead in that grave but it was more as if I didn't want our life together to end so soon.

"Molly," I said. "Remember when I told you the story about Mr. Winnipesaukee? I was on my way to work on your dad's farm but that old man didn't seem to take me for a farmer. You know what he thought I should be? You'll never guess. A teacher. I thought it was kind of funny when he said that. I mean, I was one of the worst readers in my school. The teachers were always after me for something. In fact, mostly I got into trouble. But now, it's got me to thinking. I'm not getting anywhere just working for Mr. Pike. And it isn't as if I don't like him. I think he's a great man. The problem is that I can't save up any money at all. My other problem is that I don't want to leave you, Molly. Now I know that might sound foolish to some folks but right now, I need to be close to you."

I'm not sure how all those thoughts came into my mind that night but they just kept niggling me until one day, I spoke to Mr. Pike about it. His opinion mattered to me.

I waited for several seconds while he focused his eyes on something on the wall and puffed on his pipe.

Finally, he said, "Well, I reckon that might not be such a foolish notion after all."

"Really?"

He nodded, puffed twice, and replied, "I noticed your mind ain't exactly on farming. But what makes you think you could be a teacher?"

He had me stumped there because all I really had was that suggestion from that old man down by the river. Somehow, he'd put that notion into my head.

I shook my head. "I don't know, sir. Ever since Molly died, I don't seem to know who I am or what I want."

Mr. Pike nodded and puffed on his pipe.

"That's to be understood, son. You've been through a lot of heartache the past few months. More than what some men have to endure their whole life."

I looked at him and waited to see if he had an answer for me but he seemed lost in thought.

"What do you think I should do, Mr. Pike?"

After clicking his pipe on his teeth several times, he looked at me and said, "I think, Patrick, you need to take some time off before you make a decision. I think you should go up and see your Pa."

My first thought was of Molly. I didn't want to leave her. Not yet.

"I know what you're thinking, son, but your Molly isn't going anywhere. She'll be right here when you come back. If you like, while you're gone, I can visit the grave and put some flowers down once in awhile."

I knew he was right. I also knew I was torturing myself by going up to that graveyard every week.

"You are a hard worker, Patrick, even if your heart isn't in it so I'll give you a little extra pay this month. You deserve it and it will pay for food and lodging along the way."

By the look on Mr. Pike's face, I knew the decision had been made for me. I would not only see my father again but I would be passing once more through Sarah's Valley and I was anxious to see Winnipesaukee if he was still living up in that cabin by the river.

Chapter Six

Now Mr. Pike couldn't part with his truck but he could with his old mare. In fact, he told me that she would probably find better grass to eat along the way than she would on the farm. She was more of a hindrance to him than a help.

"And she won't ever run out of gas," he said with a chuckle.

Two days later, I was ready to go. The sun was barely up and the air was still crisp when I started out. Mr. Pike was up before me and had Rosie all saddled and ready. Mrs. Pike didn't come out but I'd heard her in the kitchen and just as I mounted, she came running from the house.

"Patrick," she called, "I've fixed some vittles for you." She handed me a small knapsack. "You be careful and watch out for strangers. It's bad times right now and there's desperate men who'd steal the shirt off your back."

Somehow, when Mrs. Pike said that, it made me feel warm inside. She was a good woman down deep inside. After she said it, she raced back to the house but I thought I'd seen a tear in her eye. She and Mr. Pike never had any children so I figured her motherly instincts were showing a bit there.

I longed to go to the graveyard but it was five miles in the other direction and five miles on a horse isn't the same as five miles in a vehicle so I started riding north east. It was easy to ride across the fields because most of them were bare anyway. There were many miles of plain nothing. In good years, cattle filled that land for as far as you could see but now only dried out grass covered the ground. There was no water for livestock. Dust and tumbleweeds filled the farmers' dugouts. Even the river running through Swift Current had dried up.

I remember the dust coming off Rosie's hoofs and floating past me into the air when she was walking. Some farmers hadn't bothered to plant anything in their grain fields. Even though we'd had some rain during the past couple of years, it took the earth a while to catch up. They said 1937 was the worst year with only eight inches of rain for the whole year. When I rode through some farmyards, I could see the families had vacated their homes. It didn't take long for the weeds and drifts of fine dust to take over the yards. Those folks had piled as many of their belongings as they could into their trucks or wagons and pulled out. I knew many of them headed north, hoping to homestead and make a new beginning. Anywhere was better than trying to survive in a dust bowl.

When the sun was high above me, I stopped at one abandoned house and decided to find some shade and see what Mrs. Pike had packed for me. The north side was the coolest and there was a small patch of grass for the horse. It wasn't green but Rosie was used to eating almost anything.

Out of curiosity, I checked to see if the door was unlocked and it was. As it squeaked open, scraping against the floor, I had to stand and stare for a moment before stepping all the way inside. I felt as if I were trespassing into someone's private hell.

The homeowners couldn't have had much room in their truck or wagon for hauling away their belongings. The woman of the house had emptied her cupboards but the table still had cups and plates piled on it. The yellow cotton curtains on the windows had streaks of brown dirt clinging to them. There was a water bucket on the counter with the dipper still in it. I wandered through the kitchen and into the small living room. It faced south but the sun had a hard time trying to shine through the dust-covered windows. From where I stood, I could see the outside windowsill lined with a row of dead grasshoppers. There was an old battered rose-colored sofa with a matching chair that filled most of the room and along one wall there was, what my mother used to call a sideboard. The dust on top was about an inch thick, and behind the dirty glass, I could see several teacups with a matching teapot. It was a sad reminder of what life was like before the drought came.

I turned away and didn't want to look at anything more in the house. I imagined there were two small bedrooms upstairs and I hoped they'd had enough room to take the beds with them. All I could think about was that poor farmer's wife who had to leave so many treasures behind.

I stepped outside. The heat clung so mercilessly to a body you felt that you had to gasp for air to breathe.

Rosie didn't seem too interested in the dried out grass. She stood with her head down, resting.

I had no feeling for riding out across that dry field. It was still some ways to the main highway. It would be at least another four or five days before I would get to the Qu'Appelle Valley. And that would be making good time. From there, I figured I had about a week's ride to see my Pa … if he still lived at our homestead.

I hadn't had word from him since before Molly and I were married. He'd never answered my last letter so I didn't know if he even knew he was going to be a grandpa. In the letter he wrote not long after I'd arrived, he said that Grandpa was doing poorly and the winter was being hard on them. They were hoping for a bounty of snow but mostly they were only getting a cold north wind. The thermometer reached as cold as 60 below, he said. However, I also knew the last thing my pa was interested in doing was writing a letter. He had always let my mother do things like that. He went to school in England but after arriving in Canada, he spent all his time working on the farm and I don't think he ever got past grade four. The letter he wrote was so hard to decipher that it was painful trying to read it.

I opened the gunnysack and took out a quart sealer of homemade brown beans with chunks of pork, and wrapped in a tea towel were two thick slices of homemade wheat bread. The other jar contained water. I guess Mrs. Pike knew there might not be many places to stop for a drink. The water in the jar was so warm I was sure I could have used it to make a cup of tea. I put my hand inside again and came out with a spoon, an apple, and three of her oatmeal cookies.

The heat was unbearable with not even a hint of a breeze so I decided to go back inside. I'd made sure to loosen the cinch belt for Rosie but decided it would be better to remove the saddle altogether. Rosie nuzzled on my arm so I knew she appreciated it. Even with walking and a slow trot, her flanks were white with foamy sweat.

Inside, it was a few degrees cooler. There were no kitchen chairs so I went into the other room and sank down into the sofa. All I could smell was dust. As I ate, I could hear the scurry of animal feet above me so I knew little varmints had already settled in. At this point, I was so hungry I think they could have come down to join me and I would have kept eating. To this day, I don't think there's anything as tasty as brown beans and homemade bread. In fact, I was feeling so good I shared that apple with Rosie. That seemed to perk her up a bit too.

Out by the barn I found the well. Many wells were dry now and I presumed this one was too but after pumping until I thought my arm would fall off, I was able to get enough out for Rosie and I filled up my jar. It wasn't the cleanest water I'd ever seen but it was cold. I was able to refill the jar Mrs. Pike had given me, Rosie had a drink, and the rest of it I poured over my head and splashed some on Rosie.

I'm not sure how long it was before we found the next farmyard but it seems forever when you're so hot, tired, and hungry. As soon as Rosie saw the house and heard a cow mooing, she started into a trot. I will always remember this stop on my journey. I wish I could remember the woman's name but it was too many years ago. She had a soft spot in her heart for this young man riding in on an old worn out horse. Well, she stuffed me with so much food I didn't think I'd be able to walk out of there. If that weren't enough, she loaded me down with enough provisions to keep me going for another day. I couldn't thank her enough.

"Where'd you come from and where you heading?" her husband asked, as I was getting to leave.

"I've come from the Pike farm," I said, "And I'm heading up north to visit my Pa."

He nodded. "I know Nathan Pike. A good man." He peered at me a little closer. "You that young lad whose wife and baby died not long back?"

Well, he could have punched me in the belly. I don't know why but I thought no one would ever talk about it. Didn't people know I was drowning in sorrow?

All I could do was nod.

He nodded again. "Well, you're a strong young man. Before you know it, you'll find yourself another woman and end up with a batch of kids."

I was glad to be up in the saddle so he couldn't see my face. It would have been good for me to turn around and thank his wife again for all her kindness but the tears were running too freely down my face.

Chapter Seven

On the third night, I slept in a ditch near a big fir tree along the side of the road. There were no other trees for miles around. I knew I didn't dare go any farther because I could hear the rumble of thunder far off in the west. A storm was heading my way and even though the thought of lightning hitting that big tree frightened me, I hoped that if the lightning stopped, I could seek shelter under the branches. My hope was that Rosie wouldn't get spooked, break loose from her tether, and go running off on me.

As it happened, the thunder and lightning stayed in the west but the rain came down in buckets. I figured every farmer in Saskatchewan must be outside doing a jig. Even lying under those big branches didn't keep all the rain off me but it had been so long since I'd smelled the fresh air after a downpour that I laid there, breathing it in with all my might. Rosie must have felt about the same because she stood still with her head down and let the water run down her whole body. The saddle was under the branches with me so Rosie was enjoying a good bath.

I stayed awake as long as I could, listening to the rain pattering against the branches above my head. It was a relief that the thunder and lightning never did come close. I don't remember when I fell asleep but suddenly my eyes opened and the sun was shining. I knew this would not be enough moisture to be of any real help to the farmers. Mr. Pike said they needed about a week of steady rain so it would have time to soak into the parched earth. The ground was so dry that a rain like this would not soak down far enough to do any good. It did seem to cheer everyone up though. It was as if God still knew how to make rain.

I knew it had cheered everyone because that morning I rode through a town, whose name I can't recollect at the moment, and I saw the excitement in people's eyes. It was amazing what hope was capable of accomplishing in the human spirit. I imagine that village has gone the way of most of those small places - ghost towns now. The most prominent building back then seemed to be the schoolhouse. I had to stop Rosie so I could stop and stare. I'd been in such a gall darn hurry on my way to the Jordan ranch on the way down, that I hadn't even remembered seeing it. Now, it stood out like a something out of a history book. If I recall, it was all brick and very stately looking.

"Rosie," I said. "If I'm going to be a school teacher, this is the kind of school I want to teach in."

Of course, Rosie snorted in agreement.

I went into the only store on the street to see if I could get a few supplies. There were still large puddles sitting on the main street and a few ruts forming. Everyone in the store was talking about the rain, and even though the farmers thought the drought might be over, they figured it was good to keep praying for more.

"The Lord is testing us, He is," proclaimed one of the customers in a loud voice. There were several other people standing around. It didn't seem that any were interested in buying anything. I wasn't sure that any of them felt that the Lord was testing them either.

The man who spoke it was tall with a long black beard. The blackness started at the top of his head where a black hat was perched and went right down from there to his clothing and black boots.

"What do you think, son?" he asked in a deep booming voice.

I looked around and I appeared to be the only one he was conversing with, so I said, "About what, sir?"

"This drought," he said. "There's many a man who's lost his faith because of this. I say the Lord is testing us. You look like an intelligent young man. What do you say?"

I then had five or six men all staring at me. It appeared they were thinking they might have some fun at my expense, so I said, "It might have tested some men's faith but I'd say from personal experience that it dims in comparison to losing your wife and a baby son. That was my experience and I must admit that I am struggling to keep my faith."

73

There wasn't much left for any of them to say so they stepped aside as I made my way out of the store, carrying a sack with a few items in it. I had seen a small café across the street so decided that I would have a meal before leaving town.

Two of the men whom I'd noticed in the store, came into the café when I was about half way through my meal. One of them nodded to me and smiled. As I was getting up to leave, he came over.

"Sorry to hear you lost your wife and son," he said. "Henry likes to think of himself as some kind of preacher. I'm glad you stopped him before he got into his hell and brimstone talk."

I laughed. "Me too."

"Where are you headed? Somewhere around here?"

"No, my destination is up north but I'm making a quick stop at Qu'Appelle Valley on the way."

He looked out the window. "You're making that trek all the way on horseback?"

I nodded. "Yes sir. I'm taking most of the summer. I was working for a farmer but even with the bit of rain we've been having lately, there won't be much of a crop to bring in so he thought I should take a break. It's a chance now to visit my Pa."

The man held out his hand and we shook. "Well, I hope you have a good trip, son. My name's Ken Davidson. I'm the principal at the school here."

"You're a teacher?"

He nodded. "I am. I teach the higher grades and serve as principal too."

"That's a job I've been thinking about doing. I'm not much cut out for farming. How do you get to be a teacher, sir?"

He laughed. "Well, you do need some training. There's a Normal school in Moose Jaw where you can learn to be a teacher. There are some requirements you have to meet to take the course. What makes you think you'd like to teach school?"

Now it was my turn to laugh. "This might sound kind of foolish but I met a man a couple of years ago who thought that's what I should be. I took him for a wise person so it's been playing on my mind."

"Was he a teacher?"

"No, but that's what he always thought he would've like to be. He had no choice though as he was an orphan and just learned to survive."

"What was his name? Maybe I know him."

I shook my head. "Probably not. I'm not sure if he's still alive. That's why I'm going through Qu'Appelle Valley. I'd love to talk with him again. His name was Frank Lawdry but he called himself Winnipesaukee."

Mr. Davidson thought for a few seconds. "Somehow that name sounds familiar. Did he live in an old shack right down by the river? The government tried to get him to move but he refused. He met the RCMP with a rifle if I remember correctly. Claimed his sister owned that land and he'd shoot the first man who set his foot on it."

"That's him. He's still alive then?"

"As far as I know. I think everyone in southern Saskatchewan has heard about him. He must be over a hundred now and still living on his own."

Well, it felt like my heart was going to burst right out of my chest. If what he thought were true, I would be able to see my old friend again.

I knew if I could talk to Winnipesaukee, he would give me wise advice.

Chapter Eight

Suddenly my very existence seemed to have more purpose. This was the first time since I'd lost Molly that I was excited about anything. Imagine if I could spend time with that old man again! I probably should have had the same feeling for my father but somehow I didn't. It wasn't that I wasn't looking forward to seeing him; it was more I was dreading telling him about Molly and what had happened. My father was an upright sort of man but showing any sort of sympathy came hard to him. He believed in showing a stiff upper lip, as the English say. Pa would have the same reaction as Molly's parents except I was quite sure he wouldn't threaten to kill me. Sometimes not showing any feelings can be just as devastating.

Rosie seemed to sense the excitement or perhaps it was the cooler weather, but she set out on a trot and she kept it up for most of the day. It was easier going because clouds covered the sun and even though it was still a warm day, after so much deadly heat, it felt almost cool.

Two days later, we arrived in Moose Jaw. After living on farms and picking up supplies in small country stores, where they sold everything from bolts made of iron to bolts of cloth, this was quite an experience. The first time I went through Moose Jaw, my old car was running on about two cylinders so all I did was stop quickly to gas up and then move on. I was paranoid about being late for my first job. This time, I could wander through the city.

At the top of a large hill, I looked down and it seemed the main street went on forever. After going past rows of large two and three story distinguished looking houses, there must have been all of six blocks of businesses on both sides. I had never seen so many eateries all in one place. Folks walking on the sidewalk weren't too bothered seeing a horse and rider going by. I did get a few glances though and figured they might be worried about my horse dropping something on their clean paved road. Rosie behaved herself though and I headed down one of the side streets to see if I could tether her somewhere. I came upon an empty lot a couple of blocks east of Main Street and tethered her there. There was one large tree for shade and even some green grass so I figured she would be okay.

Moose Jaw was a bustling city to be sure. A few buildings towered over the others. One caught my eye. It said *Army and Navy*. Well, I wasn't too sure what it was but since I saw mostly women going in and coming out with parcels, I came to the conclusion that it wasn't a recruiting office. As I walked by, I could see the merchandise displayed behind the large windows. In all my life, I'd never seen a store as large as this one.

As soon as I walked inside, the mixed smell of wood varnish and new merchandise hit me right off. There was so much to take in that I hardly knew where to begin. I must have had a panicky look on my face because an older woman came up and asked if I needed any help.

"Yes, ma'am," I said. "I sure do. I don't even know where to begin."

She laughed and it reminded me of my mother's laugh.

"Are you wanting to check out the men's clothing section?" she asked.

"You mean you have a whole section just for men's clothing?"

She smiled and nodded. "Come and I'll show you."

We walked past rows and rows of women and children's clothing, and in the back corner, she stopped.

"There you are. You look around and if you don't find what you need, come and look for me."

"Is this store just for clothing?" I asked because if it was, I would be quite disappointed.

"Oh, my no! There's a basement and an upstairs. There is everything you need or want in the *Army and Navy* store," she said.

That sales woman was right. Before I knew it I had frittered away an hour, looking and examining almost everything that interested me. I did leave with something though. Just as I was walking out, I saw a display by the door. It was pocket-sized dictionaries. They were 15 cents each but I figured I could afford it. I bought two - one for myself, and one for Winnipesaukee.

The same friendly sales woman was at the cash register.

"You must be a teacher," she said. She showed such admiration in her eyes that I almost caught myself telling a lie.

I could feel my cheeks getting warm. "That's what I'm planning on," I said.

"Good for you. I wish you all the best, young man," she said, and handed me the package.

I noticed at the end of the street on the other side, there was a café and I saw the sign that said, *Ice Cream*. I hadn't eaten any ice cream in a few years. The last time was when my grandpa had taken me with him on a long journey to Meadow Lake to sell some lumber. After the transaction, we'd gone to a small restaurant and he'd bought me an ice cream cone. It was the most wonderful taste in the world to a ten year old.

Molly and I had talked about getting an ice cream cone the day after we were married but of course, that didn't happen. The ice cream reminded me of her and it took a small slice of joy out of the eating. I would loved to have seen the look on her face when she tasted it.

My ice cream cone was 3 cents and as I walked down the street eating it, I figured I'd better get out of Moose Jaw before I spent all my money. Besides, I'd wasted enough time.

Rosie was standing waiting for me and I could tell she was anxious to get moving too.

Chapter Nine

It was almost a day's ride to Regina. The old truck could have made it in less than half the time, but I was in no rush and I loved listening to the soft clop of Rosie's hooves as she trotted down the road. A few vehicles would stop and say hello. One farmer handed me his sandwich when he heard my story. He was on his way to check his crops and he said his wife always packed too much food for him. I only saw the one sandwich but I took him at his word and was pleased to have something to eat as I rode.

Riding through Regina, I saw a gas station where I could buy a sausage with a slice of bread for 5 cents so I stopped and decided that would be my last meal for the day. I piled so many onions and pickles on my plate that it ended up being a complete meal anyway. I'm not sure how the owner felt about it but what could he say? He had his nickel.

The sun was setting as we rode away from Regina so I decided it was best to stop for the night. I found a gully that seemed a good spot for sleeping and not far away was a small creek. There wasn't much water in it but enough for Rosie to get her fill and I filled my water jar. I figured if I filled it at night, the dirt and sand would sink to the bottom and I could have a half-decent drink in the morning.

Rosie never strayed and I was pleased Mr. Pike lent her to me. I couldn't have talked to a car but Rosie was easy to talk to. She would watch me as I told her about my life. I guess she could feel the sadness in my voice when I cried and talked about Molly because she would come over and sniff my face, and nibble at my hair. Yes, she was a good horse and I was starting to care for that old nag.

By late afternoon the next day, I came to the Qu'Appelle Valley. I stopped at the top of a hill and looked down. Everything I saw was brown but with patches of green here and there because of the rain. There was still life in the valley. Brown dust covered the trees alongside the narrow gravel road. However, in between some of them, I could see wild roses blooming. A town stood to the east, named after the valley, and to the north was Fort Qu'Appelle. Somewhere in between I would find Mr. Winnipesaukee.

Qu'Appelle was an unusual valley. The hills on each side of the winding river looked as if a mighty hand had come down and rolled the soil into large mounds. In between those mounds, trees grew and flourished. The valley itself was wide in most places. Where the river ran close to the hills, there was a small cabin nestled into one of those mounds. There was the place Sarah Lawdry built her last home and where her brother, Frank lived.

I nudged Rosie and we set off at a gallop. Down the steep hill we went and on until we came to an old bridge. The path leading off from the bridge along the water and heading east had to be the right one. In the short time since my first visit, it had grown over somewhat but I was sure this was the trail I was searching for.

I remembered walking behind Winnipesaukee for what seemed like miles before coming to his small cabin. This time I had Rosie so it wouldn't seem so far.

"Come on, Rosie," I said, as I urged her down into the ditch and out again to the path. The water was not moving much and it smelled almost stagnant from the heat. It was still water though and Rosie was in need of a drink. I bent down and tasted some. All I could say is that it was wet so I took a couple of swallows. Afterwards, I filled my palms and washed my face and then I bent over and splashed some over my hair. I had no idea how sweaty I smelled but I couldn't have smelled much worse than Rosie.

The trail wound its way beside the river and then, just like the first time, the small cabin hugging the hill popped up out of nowhere. I stopped and before getting down, I watched the cabin for a minute or two. There was no smoke coming out of the chimney and the only sound I heard were a few crows off in the distance. Rosie didn't want to settle down and kept prancing which was very unlike her. I was hoping there wasn't a snake or some other creature crawling along the ground.

I wasn't exactly sure what I should do. Well, I decided that even if Winnipesaukee wasn't home, I would still stop and rest up for a bit. If no one showed up within the next couple of hours, I would at least take my dirty clothes off, have a bath in the river, and put on some clean duds. I only took one change of clothes so that would be it until I arrived at my pa's house. I was also hoping Mr. Winnipesaukee might have something in his cupboard for me to munch on.

I slid down and slipped the saddle off Rosie's back. She was moving so much, I had to keep a close grip in the bridle.

"Settle down, Rosie," I said. "We're going to rest up for a bit, girl."

Rosie's eyes were rolling and I could hardly hang on to her and that's when I heard it - the sound of someone pulling a lever back and I knew without looking, someone was pointing a rifle at my back.

Chapter Ten

N ow Molly's father had shown me the barrel end of
his old hunting rifle but at least he never aimed it
at my back. This was different. I slowly raised both my arms
and of course, Rosie forsook me. I watched helplessly as
she galloped off down toward the river.

"Turn around real slow," the voice said.

I then realized it was either a boy or a grown man with a
very childlike voice. However, young or old, he was the one
holding the weapon.

I turned slowly and faced probably the youngest would-
be killer in history.

My hands went down and I started to laugh.

"Get your hands up, Mister!" the boy said and raised the
rifle butt so that if he decided to fire, it would remove
everything from my eyebrows and up.

"Listen," I said. "I'm not here to cause trouble. I stopped to see Mr. Winnipesaukee. I'm on my way north to visit my pa so I just dropped by to say hello."

"He don't know you so get going."

"Yes, he does know me and how can I get going when you scared my horse off?"

The boy's eyes drifted over to my right to see where Rosie went and at that split second, I grabbed the rifle and swung it towards him.

"So," I said. "How does it feel having an old shotgun shoved in your face? It isn't too pleasant, is it?"

The boy shrugged. "It's okay. The gun ain't loaded anyway."

I lowered the barrel and sure enough, not a shell to be seen.

Now that I wasn't concerned about being shot, I had a good look at the boy. He was about nine or ten but small for his age. He had straight black hair that hung to his shoulders but he had bright blue eyes. He looked Aboriginal but with fairer skin and of course, no Aboriginal that I'd ever known had such blue eyes. His clothes were in tatters and he was barefoot.

"Where's Winnipesaukee?" I asked.

He shrugged. "You tell me who you are and I'll go see if he wants to talk to you."

I stared at him. "Who are you?"

He stared right back. "I'm Toby Lawdry, that's who I am."

"Toby Lawdry? Where did you come from?"

"My grandmother brought me up from down south, that's where I came from."

"Where's your grandmother now?"

"She's down in our cabin farther down the river. She's dying same as Winnipesaukee's dying."

For the first time, I saw a crack in his armor. Under that toughness, there was still a little boy and that made me feel better.

"They're both dying?"

He nodded and when he lowered his head, I could see a couple of tears leak down his cheeks. He kept his head down so I wouldn't be able to see.

"I'm sorry to hear that, Toby," I said. "Where's Winnipesaukee now? Is he in the hospital?"

He kept his head down but shook his head and pointed to the cabin. As I walked past him to the cabin door, I put my hand on his shoulder.

"You best go and find my horse. Her name's Rosie and if you treat her real nice, she'll come easy."

He turned and ran towards the river. He could bring the horse back and keep his dignity too.

Chapter Eleven

I gave a couple of soft knocks and then pushed the
door open, not knowing what I might find. The room
was dim and musty. When Sarah and her Métis friends
built her cabin, they built it into the side of the hill so even
though there was no fresh air coming in, it felt much cooler
than outside. At first when I glanced round, I couldn't see
anyone. However, as my eyes adjusted to the dimness, I
caught some movement to the right. I remembered that to
my right, Sarah had her bed and in the corner next to the
door, so close I could reach out and touch it, there was a
small piano. I never had the opportunity to ask

Winnipesaukee about it but I did remember when he told his story, he said Sarah wished she had a piano. It was my opinion that he must have bought that old piano to bring back memories of his sister. Now, as the first time I'd seen it, it was covered with papers, clothing, and what looked like animal traps.

"Who's there? You're not Toby."

I looked away from the piano and saw a small withered-looking man with long white hair lying in Sarah's bed.

I walked slowly up to his bedside.

"Winnipesaukee, it is me, Patrick Smithson. I've come to visit you."

He was looking in my direction but I realized that he couldn't see anymore. I moved closer and put my hand on his arm. A worn dirty quilt covered the old man up to his chin.

"Patrick Smithson?"

"Yes, do you remember me?"

He cackled. "Of course, I remember you. You drove an old car that stopped working down by the bridge. I fixed that up for you the next morning while you were sleeping the day away."

"You did? I know that when I got to the car, it started up. You knew all along how to fix it?"

He nodded. "It wasn't much to fix."

"Why didn't you fix it when you first saw me?"

"Because I wanted some company. No one ever comes to visit."

"Maybe it's because you or Toby greets people with a gun."

He grinned but it was hard to tell because his cheeks were so sunken and his face so full of wrinkles. His lifeless eyes stared out at nothing.

"Well," I said, "I've come to visit now. My horse ran off when Toby showed up with that rifle so he's gone to fetch her back. I reckon that if you have some grub here, I can fix up something to eat. When was the last time you ate?"

"Don't worry about me. I'll be dying within the next few days anyway. You help that boy out if you can."

"Who is he, Mr. Winnipesaukee? He said his name is Toby Lawdry. He's a relative?"

The old man sighed and I wasn't sure if he had the strength to go on. For a few seconds he closed his eyes and I was wishing I hadn't asked a question.

When he spoke up, he sounded stronger.

"I was married once to this French woman. Like a fool, I followed her all over the country. She was the biggest mistake of my life. I should have come here with my sister, Sarah, but instead I left her somewhere along the trail. Somewhere out of Independence, I think." He stopped for a moment as if trying to remember. "I left Sarah, my sister, alone to look after those two orphan children. Orphans, just like Sarah and I were. The only good thing that came out of living with that French woman was the son we had together."

"You had a son? Did Sarah know?"

He slowly shook his head. "No, I never told her. I only saw that little boy for a few minutes and then he was gone."

When he said that, my heartache was back, ripping and tearing deep within me. "Your son died at birth?"

Again, he shook his head. "No, I was beaten and left for dead and the boy's mother took him away. I never saw him again."

"So who is this Lawdry who is here now?"

Winnipesaukee sighed and whispered, "You've tuckered me out, Patrick. I'll rest now and tell you later."

I patted his arm. "Okay, Winnipesaukee. I'll try to find something for us to eat. Maybe I can clean the cabin up a bit too."

The old man's eyes opened again. "Don't worry about me. I don't have much time left. Watch out for that little boy, Patrick. He's an orphan too."

Chapter Twelve

I sat and waited until Winnipesaukee's breath was slow and even and then I left him. Toby and Rosie were back and when I looked out the window, I saw Toby forking some hay from behind a small shed and throwing it out on the ground. Rosie would be quite happy to stay now.

Between the dying man's bed and the tiny kitchen was another narrow wooden bed, piled high with many things: work clothes, blankets, old newspapers, and peeping out here and there were several books. An old gray army blanket draped over a rope and held up with clothespins, gave Winnipesaukee some privacy.

I made my way between the wall and the beds to the far side of the cabin. It was hard to know where to begin in the kitchen. Even though the day had been warm, the air was cooling down and soon the sun would go behind one of those large hills so I needed to build a fire in the old iron cook stove. There was plenty of paper for starting it but I had to go outside to find some kindling and wood.

Toby met me as I was coming out.

"Is he dead now?"

"No, Mr. Lawdry is still alive."

He gazed up at me. "When you're finished burying him, will you bury my grandma?"

"Your grandmother is dead?"

He shook his head but then changed his mind and shrugged.

"Maybe not yet but soon. I was there this morning and she said she couldn't take it much longer. She's trying to find a home for me but I don't think she'll find one. Do you know of anyone who would want me?"

Chapter Thirteen

I didn't have an answer for the child so I changed the subject.

"Where's the woodpile? I'll need to cut up some kindling and get a fire started so we can have some supper."

He pointed to the east side of the house.

"Or, is your grandmother expecting you home?" I asked.

He shook his head. "No, she knows I stay with Winnipesaukee sometimes. She doesn't worry; I think she wants to die alone."

"Are you saying that Winnipesaukee needs someone to be with him but your grandmother doesn't?"

He shrugged. "I guess."

While I cut some kindling and carried some smaller logs to the house, Toby went back to caring for Rosie. It seemed that he felt sorry for sending her off in such a flurry so he was trying to make up for it.

It was easy to get the fire burning but not so easy trying to find any food to eat. It looked like the old man hadn't been able to get any food supplies for quite some time.

The cupboard was almost empty of everything but I did find an unopened can of pork and beans and a can of Campbell's tomato soup. There were two white chipped plates that were more gray than white, a white soup bowl with flowers on it that was covered in tiny cracks, and two coffee mugs both with handles broken off. Sitting on the stove was a teakettle with water in it and a tin saucepan. I wasn't sure how long the water had been sitting there so I poured it into the saucepan to wash it out and took the tea kettle out to Toby.

"Where's the well, Toby? I'll need some water for supper and washing the dishes."

Toby pointed to the river.

"You drink that dirty river water?" I asked, remembering all the coffee I'd consumed on my first visit.

He nodded. "You got to boil it first. That's what Winnipesaukee says."

I handed him the kettle. "Would you bring some water up for me, please?"

"Sure." He grabbed the kettle out of my hand, looked back at Rosie, and said, "Come on, Rosie."

Rosie obediently trailed behind him.

I'd used the water from the kettle to wash out the saucepan and then threw the water outside. It took a few minutes to find a can opener. Finally, I put the pan on the stove to warm up the beans. Some of the soup would be for Winnipesaukee and the remainder I would put in with the beans. The only other pan of any sort was the old frying pan that I remembered from my first visit. It was cast iron and as black as Satan.

When Toby brought the water, I boiled it for a few minutes and then mixed the can of the soup with the river water. I couldn't help wonder how many bugs and tadpoles might have lived there before we drank it. Was he dying of some disease besides old age or was he starving to death? Was there no one in the community who could come and care for an old man, even if only to bring him some decent food?

When Toby returned with more water, I asked him about it.

"He don't take things from anyone."

"But he needs food to eat. Is there no one who wants to come and bring him food?"

"One man came a while back but when Winnipesaukee pointed the rifle at him, he left and he's never come back."

"Well, do you blame him? Why won't the old man let them help him?"

"Cause he's afraid they'll take him away from his land. This here's Sarah's valley and he has to stay here until he dies. That's what he says. Then, he wants me to have it."

I looked down at the boy. There were a few things in life that this young lad would have to learn.

"I don't think this land really belongs to him, Toby. He doesn't have anything to pass on to anyone else. The government has obviously allowed him to squat here but once he dies, this will all be torn down."

"Do you know that for sure?"

I shook my head. "I don't know it for sure but that's what I think."

Tears came to his eyes. "Don't tell him that, okay?"

I shook my head. "No, I won't."

"He doesn't understand lots of things. I think he likes to live in the old days."

I smiled. "Yes, I think he does. But don't worry; I'll see if I can find a place for you."

The tears now came down and there was no stopping them. He cried like the little boy that he was and hugged me around my waist.

After he'd sniffed and wiped his nose along his sleeve, he said, "Do you think you could take me with you up to see your pa?"

Now this was something that I wasn't planning or expecting. This was my time to heal from my broken heart, to be alone and feel sorry for myself. Did I want to be responsible for the life of a young boy? A boy I didn't know and a boy who had no home to go to? Did I not have enough with which to deal?

"I suppose I could but we'll see what your grandmother says," I said, because what else could I say?

"She won't mind because she's dying and then she won't have to worry about me."

Chapter Fourteen

I believe that having someone in the house perked Winnipesaukee up. He was able to sit up and swallow a few teaspoons of soup. Toby and I finished a half can of beans each in record time and wished for more. I would have given almost anything to have a piece of bread but there was none to be found.

Winnipesaukee felt more comfortable in a sitting position so I placed the pillow behind him.

"Are you feeling better?" I asked.

"No," he said. "I am still dying whether I sit or lie down. It is easier for me to breathe this way though. Before I die, Patrick, I want to tell you about Toby."

I pulled a chair up and sat close to the bed.

"He isn't here with us, is he?"

"No, he's out with Rosie, my horse."

He giggled. "I didn't think he was here. I couldn't smell him." He continued chuckling. "He always wonders how I know he's in the room but I never tell him."

I stared down at the withered old man who still kept his sense of humor and could even laugh like a child.

"What about him?" I asked. "How is he related to you?"

He cleared his throat. His voice was only above a whisper but it was clear and easy to understand.

"I told you I was once married to a French woman. We were together for a few years but when she got pregnant, she was upset. We were living off other people, Patrick. It is not a part of my life that I am proud of."

"You mean you were stealing from people?"

He nodded. "And worse. I won't go into detail but if the truth be known, I would have and should have spent all of my days in prison. Some folks might have thought hanging was too good for me."

"You did this for a woman?"

He nodded. "Yes, it sounds crazy, doesn't it? I could not believe the hold that woman had on me. She was a few years older than I was and a woman of the world. She taught me about life but not in a good way. When she gave birth to our son, she had me beaten and left for dead. Now

I have learned that she gave the child away but years later when the lad was grown, he searched to find his real identity and discovered he was Tobias Lawdry. At least, the woman had the decency to give the child my name."

"That was Toby's father?"

"Grandfather. I don't know the name of Tobias' son but it appears that I am little Toby's great great grandfather."

"That's a big title."

He grinned. "I don't mind being called grandpa but the rest is too much. It makes me sound old."

"Who checked all this out?"

"His mother and grandmother searched the Lawdry family name. It took them to Montana. Some place by Milk River close to the Saskatchewan border. That's where Sarah lived for several years. From there, they discovered that she had moved to this valley. They had no idea that Sarah was dead and that I was here until they arrived."

"Doesn't it seem strange that they would come all the way here to find someone with the same name? Surely, they realized how old Sarah would be. It doesn't make sense to me. Does it to you?"

The old man started to laugh but ended up choking so I quickly got up, raised him higher, and patted his back. In a few minutes, he was ready to continue his story.

"I guess this was their last hope. Maybe they thought Sarah had married and had family. The ones who knew of her spoke highly of her, saying she was a teacher who could speak English, French, and Algonquin. Apparently, this impressed them."

"Where was Toby's grandfather?"

"I was told he went to war and never returned."

"So your son was raised by adoptive parents but when he was older he searched to find his real identity. He must have decided to keep the Lawdry name. You don't know his son's name but his grandson was Tobias Lawdry and Toby is named after him."

"That sounds about right. I don't know what happened to Toby's mother but by the time they arrived here, there were just the two of them. Last winter was hard on the grandmother. She caught pneumonia and has never recovered. Maybe a warm dry summer will help her."

"Toby says she's dying."

He smiled. "The boy has had too much death in his family. Now he thinks everyone is dying."

"Are you feeling better?"

"I feel better that you came. I would like you to check on Toby's grandmother. Maybe if you look after Toby for a while, she can get better. She is too sick to run after a child and he needs someone to watch him before he turns into a little animal."

I laughed. "I can do that for you, Winnipesaukee. You helped me out once so now it is my turn to repay you. I'll ride over to the little town tomorrow and bring you some supplies too."

He grunted. "I won't be in need of supplies but the boy and his grandmother will. Go, take the boy, and check on her. When you come back, there is something I want to give to you."

I helped him settle back down and by the time I had cleaned up the kitchen and walked past him, he was already asleep.

Toby and I walked along the path to his grandmother's cabin. It was a cloudy cool day and dark clouds were gathering once again in the west. Perhaps the reports were true - the drought was finally over. How many years, I wondered, would it take for the land to be green and rich again?

Chapter Fifteen

It took about twenty minutes of fast walking to reach her house. Toby talked nonstop all the way. Rosie, I saw, was following us in the distance. She seemed to be acting more like a dog than a horse.

"What's your grandmother's name?" I asked Toby.

He stopped walking and looked at me in a dumbfounded way.

"And I don't mean Grandma," I said. "What do other people call her?"

He grinned. "Lilly."

Lilly was sitting in a rocking chair on the veranda when we walked up. She'd closed her eyes and she seemed to be sleeping.

"Let's not wake her," I whispered to Toby. "If she's not feeling well, it's best that she gets her sleep."

He walked up closer and stared at her.

"She ain't sleeping; she's dead," he said, in a definite tone. His face was as serious as an eighty year old announcing someone's demise.

With that, her eyes flew open and she struggled to sit up straight.

"What's going on, Toby? Who are you, mister?" She turned to her grandson. "Have you got yourself in trouble again?"

She looked up at me. It was hard to tell her age because you could see she wasn't a well woman. She could have been forty or sixty. Her hair wasn't gray yet but there were lines in her skin and she was so thin that her clothes simply hung on her.

Unlike Winnipesaukee's cabin, this building was not built into the hill. It was L - shaped with worn shingles that needed replacing, and gray siding that had seen better days. There was nothing pretty or inviting about it at all. The yard was mostly weeds and although there was a window box under what I thought was the kitchen window, there were no flowers in it, only stinkweed and dandelions.

"Ma'am, "I said, "My name is Patrick Smithson. I came to visit Mr. Winnipesaukee and that's where I met Toby."

"You were visiting Frank Lawdry? He didn't shoot you on sight?" She laughed but it started her coughing and it took a few minutes before she could stop. "Sorry," she said.

"I should learn not to laugh too hard. It gets me coughing every time."

"Is there anything I can get you? Do you need some type of syrup or perhaps honey for your cough? I'm going into town tomorrow to get some supplies so I can get you whatever you need."

She smiled. "That's kind of you but it seems nothing helps. I hope Toby hasn't been a bother." She looked at her grandson with a mixture of love and exasperation in her eyes.

"No, he's been no problem. Mr. Lawdry asked if I'd see what you might need. He sure doesn't have much in his cupboard. I hope you have more."

She wanted to laugh but I could see she stopped herself and she smiled.

"I'd hardly know where to start. What did you say your name was?"

"Patrick Smithson, ma'am."

"Well, Patrick, if I could have some fresh apples, a few potatoes, and some flour, I'd be very pleased."

"That's no problem. I'll head out first thing in the morning."

She struggled to get up. Her legs were so thin I thought she would just topple over backwards.

"Just wait, Patrick, and I'll get you some money."

"Ma'am, there's no need. I think I'll have enough and when I come back, you can pay me then."

She looked relieved as she sank back into the rocking chair again.

"Did you want Toby to stay here with you?"

She shook her head. "There's no need. I mostly just sit here and sleep. This is no life for a boy but the doctor said that rest is the only thing that can cure me." She pushed a string of hair off her face. "He seems to enjoy going over to Frank's place and I know Frank doesn't approve of any nonsense."

"That's true but Winnipesaukee isn't doing all that well right now. He's mostly sleeping. Toby could keep an eye on him when I leave to get supplies. I can put him to work cleaning up the yard."

"Thank you, Patrick."

"You're all right here by yourself?"

She nodded. "Toby is usually over there with his old grandpa anyway." She pointed to the door. "There's some bread on the table if you and the boy are hungry. "

She closed her eyes so I knew that as soon as we'd had something in our stomachs it would be time to leave.

I wasn't sure how much I was getting myself into but it seemed that every time I opened my mouth, I was getting more involved. All I'd wanted to do was have a little visit with Winnipesaukee, perhaps spend the night, and then get an early start the next morning.

My plans changed once again when I went into the cabin

Chapter Sixteen

I was standing and looking at the body when Toby walked in and stood beside me. I glanced down at him. He was staring at his grandfather with a bewildered look.

"Winnipesaukee is dead," I said.

He nodded. "I knew he would die today."

"No one knows when someone is going to die, Toby. Even doctors can't say for sure. Sometimes old people live longer than what you think. Even Winnipesaukee didn't know."

He looked up at me, his eyes wide and so blue it was like looking into a deep pool of water. "No," he said. "I knew this morning that the old man was going to die."

I decided it was not the time to argue with a child, so I said, "It's okay to cry. Do you feel like it?"

He shook his head. "I cried this morning. I'm okay now." He walked over and touched Winnipesaukee's sunken cheek. "His skin is still warm," he said. "He must have just died."

I stared at this young boy and wondered what to do with him - what to do with him and the body in the bed.

"Do you want to go home now, Toby?" I asked. "Perhaps you should go and tell your grandmother. I think she might like that."

He shook his head. "No, now we must bury Winnipesaukee."

My first inclination was to tell him that he was the child; I was the adult and thus, he should be doing what I say but somehow, I couldn't. The little boy looking up at me seemed so wise beyond his years.

"I think," I said, "We have to let someone know that he has died before we bury him. I know he wanted to be buried down where Sarah is buried but that might not be possible. A person can't bury dead bodies anywhere they please."

"I promised him," he said.

"Well, I know you did, Toby, but you don't understand the laws of the land yet."

For the first time, I saw tears forming in his eyes.

"He will be very disappointed if we don't do as he asked."

"Maybe he would be if he were alive but he'd dead. He won't know where he's buried."

The tears ran down his cheeks.

"But I will," he said, folding his arms over his chest. "I will be breaking my promise to my grandfather."

What more could I say? How do you reason with such a child? How do you tell him that sometimes promises are broken - like promising my Molly that I would care for her and protect her from all harm for the rest of my life? Who was I to tell a young boy about not having to keep a promise?

The sun was down now. I wasn't sure of the time but I thought it must be close to Toby's bedtime. Although, unlike me when I was a child, I doubted Toby was on any sort of schedule at all. My parents and grandparents made certain that everything was done in an orderly fashion, even going to bed at the proper time. And stopping all work at four to break for a cup of tea. Or, as my grandma used to say 'a cuppa.'

"Well, we can't bury him tonight because it's too dark. We'll have to wait until morning. I can walk you home and then in the morning we can bury Winnipesaukee."

There was a touch of a smile on his lips but I knew it wasn't everything that he wanted to hear.

"I will stay here tonight, Patrick," he said. "This is the last time I can stay with him. I'm the only one that can carry on his name."

I stared down at him. "Who are you?" I said, "Are you really an old man disguised in a child's body?"

With that, he started to laugh but soon the laughter turned to tears and he collapsed in my arms. I carried him over to the bed behind the old blanket divide and he cried until he fell into an exhausted sleep. I gently laid him down and covered him.

It was so dark in the cabin now, I could hardly see where I was going, but I managed to find my way to Winnipesaukee's bed and pull the blanket over his face. There he could spend his last night. Tomorrow was another day and I didn't even want to think about it or what I was planning on doing.

Before trying to find space beside Toby to sleep, I went outside and built a fire in the old fire pit. Rosie walked over and stood, watching. I think she was waiting for Toby and when he didn't show up, she went back to sleeping by the shed.

The light from the fire flickered through the cabin windows and made me feel better. I don't remember falling asleep but when I awoke, it was morning and sunlight filled the room. Toby was gone and I almost dreaded looking on the other side of the curtain.

Surely, the child could not have carried the body down to the river. It was a relief to see that Winnipesaukee's body was still there; however, the blanket was off his face. Toby must have wanted it that way so I left it.

I went outside to get the fire started. There were still warm coals from the night before so soon flames were leaping up and licking the sides of the kindling. The sun was not high in the sky so it was still early. I figured about seven. If any other child were missing, I would have been sick with worry. Already I believed this boy was different than most his age.

Without looking at Winnipesaukee, I went into the kitchen area to see what I could make for breakfast. In the bottom of an old canister, there were enough grounds to make a pot of coffee. Other than that, I could find nothing. That meant that if we were going through this burial ceremony, I would have to go into the town to buy some supplies. No matter what I was going to do, we would need some food.

I put the grounds in the saucepan because the coffee pot that sat out by the fire pit probably hadn't been cleaned since the first day Winnipesaukee had used it. There was still water from the day before and the sediment had settled on the bottom so I poured that over the grounds.

The day was warm and there were no sounds except for a few birds flying over and the occasional mourning sound of a loon from the distance. As I lifted the pan to place it over the fire, I heard a strange sound coming from somewhere down by the river. Rosie snorted and her ears came forward.

It was a strange sound but it was one that I'd heard before. I remembered hearing it when Winnipesaukee told me his life story that night sitting out in front of the fire. It seemed like a lifetime ago but it had been only two years. Now I knew where Toby was. He was down by the river singing the Death Song - the song of the Abenaki. *Ya ni go we ya. Ni go we.*

The sound of the child's voice singing his dirge travelled far over the water. Somewhere in the distance, a loon called and another answered. I stopped and listened, transformed. The water hushed as it slowly wound its way through the valley. Now and again, it lapped gently against the shore or gurgled as it bubbled over rocks almost hidden below the surface. The breeze softy touched my face and the air smelled fresh and clean. This was the day Toby Lawdry and I would bury Winnipesaukee. This was the day Sarah's valley would be gone forever.

Chapter Seventeen

I am not sure how long I stood and watched and listened. Perhaps for only a few minutes but it seemed timeless. Never would I forget the sound of that child's voice and seeing him on his knees, eyes lifted to the heavens. The memory of it still sends chills down my body.

I shuffled my way back, too weak to pick my feet up, and went to the small shed that stood beside the house. The door was hanging on only one rusty hinge. I lifted it and pulled it open. The place smelled dusty and close. Ancient rusted tools of all sorts were scattered over the shed floor. Along one wall hanging on a nail was a spade. I took it down and headed back to the boy. I had no idea what or if this is what I should be doing. As I look back, I realize that even though I was a widower and my wife had bore my dead child, I was only a lad myself.

By this time, Toby had stopped singing and was sitting, Indian-style, looking out over the water. How someone so young could have such an aged heart, I could not comprehend. The boy looked up as he heard me approaching.

"You took a long time to get here, Patrick," he said.

What was I to say? I wasn't called upon to dig someone's grave every day.

"I'm sorry," I said. I bent down and laid my hand on the top of his head. "I'm sorry about Winnipesaukee."

He nodded. "It's okay. He lived a long life and it was time for him to leave."

"What do you mean, leave?"

Toby shrugged. "I don't know. That's what people say when someone dies. Winnipesaukee told me he was just going to die. That's all. Just die."

He stood up and slapped the grass and dirt from the back of his pants with his one hand.

"Well," he said. "I suppose we ought to get busy and bury him."

"I'm not sure about this. What if we can't dig the hole deep enough and he washes out? Maybe we should check with someone in town to see if he can be buried in the cemetery there."

A look of horror passed over his face. "Be buried with all those people who hated him? I thought Winnipesaukee was your friend?"

"He was but we still have to do things the right way."

Toby crossed his arms over his chest and with his lower lip trembling, he said, "The right way is to have him beside his sister. If you won't do it, I will. I promised him and I won't break my promise. If you don't want to help, Patrick

116

Smithson, you can keep riding. Me and Winnipesaukee don't need you anyway."

I looked down at the stubborn little boy and thought of the old man whose body lay stretched out in the bed inside the cabin and knew what I had to do. Winnipesaukee's heart was with his sister, Sarah, and that's where he had to stay.

"Where is Sarah buried?" I asked.

Toby smiled. "I'll show you," he said, and turned down the path.

It wasn't too far away. Perhaps about half way from Winnipesaukee's cabin to his grandmother's house. I was relieved to see that it was quite a ways from the river. I'd had visions of digging by the water, having the grave fill in, and seeing the old man's skeleton drifting downstream.

Sarah's grave was in a peaceful spot close to a tree. If the river were high, the water would almost reach the gravesite but not quite. After suffering such a drought for so many years now, the burial spot seemed far off and almost desolate.

A carving in the old tree marked the grave spot. The tree itself would not last much longer. Bark was beginning to peel away and most of the limbs did not produce leaves anymore. It had been majestic in its day but like old Winnipesaukee, it was ready to rest in peace.

Other than the crude carving in the bark that said *Sarah's Valley*, there was no sign of any grave.

"How do you know this is where her grave is?" I asked.

"My grandfather told me. He told me that I must make sure he was buried here too. After he is buried and I sing another song, we have to burn down his cabin."

I stared at him.

"What do you mean, burn down his cabin? We are already probably committing a crime by secretly burying him, now you want me to commit arson?"

He shrugged. "I don't know what that means, but that's what the old man told me and I have to do what he said."

"He said you have to sing a song?"

"Well, no but I want to do that. He taught me the song and said that all Abenaki sing that when someone dies."

"Yes, I know. He told me that, too."

"He did?"

"Yes, he kept me up all night telling me the story of his life. Did he tell you the story too?"

He shook his head and I noted a fleeting sadness pass over his face. I wished I hadn't told him but I couldn't take the words back.

"I know he would've told you if you were older. It was a story much too long and too sad to tell a young boy."

"Was it always a sad life for Winnipesaukee?"

"No, there were happy times too. Did you know he went almost all across America with a wagon train?"

He shook his head. "Were those the happiest times?"

"I believe it started out that way but it was on the wagon trail that Sarah and Frank lost both their parents."

"Lost? How did they lose their parents?"

"It's just an expression. I meant they both lost their lives on that journey so Sarah and Frank were on their own."

"Who's Frank?"

"You know, that's what your grandmother calls Winnipesaukee. That was Winnipesaukee's real name. Frank Lawdry. That was his name when he was born. Their mother died first but later on, a mudslide enveloped the whole wagon train and killed everyone, including their father. So the two children had to keep going all on their own."

"How come they didn't die with everyone else?"

"Because it was raining so hard, the two children pulled their wagon off the trail and crawled underneath to keep from getting so wet. No one saw them and when the train followed the trail that ran under a mountain, the rocks and mud gave way and covered everyone and everything."

"And they were left all alone?"

I nodded.

"That is like me." He looked up at me with a solemn stare. "I am all alone too."

I realized there was no point reassuring him that he still had his grandmother since he believed she would soon be dying too. Sometimes, as my father always said, if you can't lick them, join them.

"I suppose you are but if you are anything like Frank and Sarah Lawdry, you will be strong and courageous too."

He probably didn't understand the meaning of courageous but I could tell he liked the sound of it. A smiled played on the corner of his lips.

"Maybe I'll call myself Winnipesaukee," he said, with a grin.

I grinned down at him. "As Winnipesaukee once told me, all warriors must earn their good names."

His eyes grew big. "Was Winnipesaukee a warrior?"

"I believe he thought of himself as one. After all, he did stand his ground and wouldn't let anyone take his home away from him."

"Why did he tell me to burn it?"

"Perhaps, because those old times are gone."

"Was this the only place where Winnipesaukee was happiest?"

"Yes, I believe so."

Before we began the burial, we walked back to the cabin, sat down by the fire, and had a cup of very strong coffee. I knew my mother had never let me drink coffee when I was that age but somehow Toby was a different child. Besides, I had nothing else to give him. When we were finished drinking in silence, I stood up and threw the leftover grounds at the bottom of my cup into the brush. Toby followed suit.

I could delay no longer. The day was heating up and I had no idea how long it would take for a body to begin to smell.

Without speaking, I picked my spade back up and Toby headed for the shed where he found a rusty shovel.

Neither of us rushed as we walked along the old path by the river. For me, it seemed we reached the burial place too quickly.

We both stood and looked around for the best spot for Winnipesaukee's final resting place. It sounded inviting describing it that way.

"Here's the best place for Winnipesaukee," Toby said.

It was at an angle from the other grave spot and facing east.

"It is a good spot," I said. "Why did you choose here?"

"So Winnipesaukee can wake up to the sun."

"You know he's dead, Toby. That's what he told you. He's not going to see the sun."

He shrugged. "My grandmother says that someday the dead will wake up and the world will be good again. It will be a paradise. If that's true, I want him to wake up and see the sun in the morning."

I smiled and nodded. "I think that's a lovely thought. We will bury him facing east."

It took all morning with many breaks and trips down to the river for drinks but we finally completed our job. I discovered that Toby was a tireless worker. He was still a child though and could not keep going on a stomach filled only with strong coffee.

"Before we bring Winnipesaukee here," I said. "I think we should have some food in our stomachs. If we don't eat soon, one of us might pass out."

"Not me," he said, stubbornly. "I can keep going. We must finish everything in one day."

"Toby, we are only human beings; we have to stop to eat."

He sighed. "There's a clump of saskatoon bushes not far."

"I think the berry season is over, Toby. They're probably all dried up by now or the birds have eaten them."

He shook his head. "No, I saw them. They were all gone but after the rain, they started to grow again."

It was a five-minute walk away. The bushes were so full of berries that from a distance, they looked more blue than green. After ten minutes of silent eating, Toby said, "I didn't know I was so hungry." He looked over at me and grinned. His lips, teeth, fingers, and the front of his shirt were stained purple with berry juice.

We could delay the burial no longer. Either we put Winnipesaukee in the ground or we had to find someone else to bury him.

Toby must have dreaded the thought of it too because he didn't seem to be in such a rush to bury his grandfather now. Sometimes I would glance back from the path and see him several feet behind me.

"Toby," I said, as I stopped and waited for him to catch up, "Are you going to help me or do you want me to do this all by myself?"

His eyes filled with tears. "I didn't want him to die, Patrick."

I walked back and put my arm around his shoulder. "I know but when a person gets that old, it just happens. We have to move on."

"But where am I going to move on to? I don't have a sister like Sarah to be with me."

I patted the top of his head. "Don't worry," I said. "I'll make sure you are looked after."

Chapter Eighteen

Before lifting Winnipesaukee out of the bed, I wrapped the blanket around him. He was so thin and weighed so little, it was like lifting up a small child. His head fell against my chest and his white hair touched my chin. I could not stop the tears from coming. How often I had thought about Molly and wished I could have held her in my arms one last time. She looked so peaceful lying there in the bed but someone had dragged me away so I never looked upon that beautiful face again.

Once again, Toby and I walked down the path. He walked in front and I followed, carrying Winnipesaukee in my arms. There were no sounds in the air. It was as if all the creatures that lived nearby were paying homage to the dead man. It felt like a long journey that would never end.

I gently dropped the old man's body into the hole that we had dug. He was so emaciated that I needn't have worried about it not being large enough for the body. I reached down and covered his face with the old blanket.

Both of us looked into the grave with tears streaming down our cheeks. Neither one of us wanted to say goodbye.

"Patrick," Toby said, as he wiped a tear from his cheek, "I think you should say a prayer."

I shook my head. "I'm sorry but I cannot. Death is too fresh for me right now and I don't think God wants to hear from me."

He looked at me for a few moments and then said, "Maybe I should sing the death song then before we cover him over."

I nodded. "That would be good."

I watched in wonder as the small boy with long black hair and blue eyes went down on his knees and looking heavenward, began his song.

Ya ni go we ya. Ni go we ... the song went on and on. Whether the words were truly Abenaki, I do not know, but they were sung with such sweet sadness, the sentiments were clear.

We covered Winnipesaukee with the soft dirt from the bank of the river and I knew this was the end of a generation. Sarah's valley would be no more. In a few years, the old tree would rot away and no one would even know that there were two burial places there beside the slow meandering river.

We walked back to Winnipesaukee's cabin, each deep in our own thoughts. We could hear Rosie calling us as we neared the old building. I had tethered her before we left and she was anxious to go to the river for a drink.

"Why don't you take her down for a drink, Toby?" I asked.

He nodded. "If you want to burn the cabin while I'm there, that's okay with me," he said.

"It's one thing to burn the cabin but what if all the grass starts on fire too? Everything around here is bone dry. Then what would we do?" I asked.

"I don't know. That's what Winnipesaukee wanted. That's all I know."

"Well, let's think about it first before we do anything. The old man said he was going to give me something but he didn't get the chance. I think I should search through the place to see what it might have been. Maybe it was something for you, Toby."

His eyes lit up. "Do you think so? I would like to have something from him."

"Go down to the river with Rosie. I'll look through the house."

I hesitated by the door as I had at the old abandoned farmhouse. I suddenly felt like an intruder. Everything inside belonged to another person who was not with us anymore. That spot in my life he had filled, no matter how small, was gone forever.

The inside was stifling and so gloomy that the first thing I did was part the curtains to let in some sunlight. There was no point in leaving the door open to let the outside air in because it was hot with no breeze. The curtain was so fragile it ripped in my hand. I pulled it down, rolled it up, and went out and threw it in the fire pit. Maybe Toby would be satisfied if we burned everything from inside Winnipesaukee's cabin but didn't destroy the buildings. I was hoping to convince him it would be easier to set it on fire in the winter when there would be no worry about setting all of southern Saskatchewan ablaze.

After putting the curtains from the cabin's only three windows into the pit, I started on the bedding. From there, I moved over to the piano and everything piled on it that would burn, I tossed out the door.

One thing for certain, I could never chop up that little piano and throw it into the fire. While I was standing and admiring it, Toby walked in.

"We can't burn that, can we?"

I shook my head. "No, someone could find lots of enjoyment playing that old thing. Do you know anyone who would want it?"

"No, I don't know anyone."

"Do you know what I think we should do, Toby?"

"No, what?"

"Since your grandmother is so sick..."

"She's dying."

"Maybe she is but right now, she's just sick and is trying to get well."

He shoved his hands into his pockets.

"No, she's dead now."

"Well, when we're finished cleaning some of the things up here, we'll go and check on her. If she isn't dead, maybe you can come with me to go and meet my pa. Then, when we get back, we can figure out what to do with Winnipesaukee's cabin. By that time, there won't be such a risk of fire and we can burn the buildings down. What do you say?"

He shrugged. "I guess so. We'll have to figure out what to do with my grandma though. She can't be buried beside Winnipesaukee and Sarah."

"We'll figure that out when we see her. Right now, you can help me carry some of this stuff out … like all these newspapers, so we can burn them. Okay?"

He nodded. "Okay."

It took most of the afternoon just burning old clothes and newspapers. I checked through everything and still hadn't seen anything of importance. At least, nothing that was important enough to pass on to anyone.

It was almost four and I was starving again.

"It's time to go and see your grandmother now, Toby," I said. "We've had a long day and maybe she has something for us to eat. I feel bad that I didn't get her supplies."

He shook his head. "No, she's dead but we can cook up something for ourselves."

On the walk there, I tried to tell him that just because Winnipesaukee died, it didn't mean that his grandmother had died too but it was of no use. He was convinced that she was gone also. When we reached the fresh graveside, we stopped for a moment and looked at it. Soon the grass would cover it over and no one would even know someone was lying down below.

As we opened the door to his grandmother's house, Toby stood in the entrance and stared. There was his grandmother as alive as could be.

"You aren't dead, grandma?" he said, as if he were staring at an apparition.

She turned and laughed. "Toby, shame on you! You have to stop talking like that." She looked at me. "What have you two been up to all day? Are you hungry?"

I nodded. "Maybe after we've had our supper, we can tell you about our day."

As it turned out, Toby's grandmother was feeling better than she had in many days. When Toby went outside to bring in some wood for the stove, she told me it was because she didn't have to worry about Toby all day.

"It isn't easy for a woman my age to be running after a young boy and Toby isn't like any other child," she said. "I worry so much about him especially when he spends so much time over at Frank Lawdry's place. I'm not sure that old man is a good influence on him. He tells him tales that give him bad dreams at night. It was that old man that put the thought in his head that we were both dying." She looked out the window and watched as Toby started back to the house. "That old coot will probably outlive all of us." Toby was inside before I could answer her.

Chapter Nineteen

I f Grandma Lilly was shocked, she didn't show it.
Perhaps, she was relieved Winnipesaukee was gone
and buried. It meant she didn't have to get involved and try
to deal with figuring out what to do with the old man's
body.

A kind neighbor had brought foodstuffs over so we sat
down to the first cooked meal I'd had since dining at the
one farmer's place along the way. Lilly talked almost
nonstop in between coughing fits, and Toby and I ate
nonstop.

"You are welcome to spend the night," she said.
"There's an old shed out back that's clean and I can give
you some blankets. And, Toby," she said, "you are sleeping
in your own bed tonight."

I thanked her but said that I'd like to go back to
Winnipesaukee's place to do a bit more cleaning up.

"There's a lot to get rid of and I don't want people getting in there and taking things."

"Is there anything worth taking?"

I shook my head. "I don't think so but I wouldn't want anyone reading personal papers or things like that. It just doesn't seem right."

She nodded. "Maybe if you find something Toby might like when he gets older, you could keep it for him."

Lilly was starting to look tired. Her face was ashen and I noticed her hands starting to shake.

"You go to bed, Miss Lilly. I'll clean up here and then head back. If I find anything, I'll bring it in the morning before I leave."

"Patrick, I'm going to ask a mighty big favor. Is there any way Toby could go with you? I am at my wit's end. He needs someone watching him and I am still not well. If I just had a few weeks to rest, I know I could cope. None of the women around here want to look after him because he's such a wild child." She stopped and started coughing. I thought her lungs were going to explode as she bent over the slop pail by the end of the cook stove. Finally, after clearing her lungs of phlegm, she straightened up but held onto the corner of the cupboard for support. Tears rolled down her cheeks from all the exertion.

"Don't worry," I said. "I'll look after Toby. I've already invited him to come with me."

Again, because what else could I say?

132

It was dark by the time I got back to the cabin. The moon shone so brightly, I could see my way without any problems at all. There was something very wonderful about the valley and the river - almost magical. I could see why Sarah picked this out as the place where she wanted to live. As I walked along, following the river, I thought back on the story Winnipesaukee had told me that night when I visited him. It seemed so far back in time. So much had happened to me since then. After I returned from my father's home and brought Toby back, that would be the last time I would see this part of Saskatchewan again.

There were still live coals in the fire pit so I added some rolled up newspapers and wood and in a few minutes, it came roaring to life. I threw out most of the grounds from the bottom of the saucepan and decided making a pot of coffee was the right thing to do. This would be my tribute to Frank Winnipesaukee Lawdry. How I wished I'd had just a few more hours to spend with him.

I reused the remaining coffee grounds and after a few minutes of boiling, it turned out to be almost as strong as the one Winnipesaukee made me when I first visited him. He would have been proud. As I sat on the same rock, drinking my coffee, watching the fire, and listening to the ripples in the river and the moaning call of a loon, I thought about that long story he had told me.

There was emptiness inside me and I hoped there would be no more deaths in my life for a while. I tossed the leftover coffee grounds out and went back into the cabin.

I had cleared everything from off the piano and I knew where the piano belonged. I would somehow get it over to Toby's grandmother in the morning. That looked like the only thing in the cabin that was worth anything so Toby should have it. It would mean staying an extra day but as much as I wanted to leave, I also wanted to stay. It would be good for Toby to have something in his life that resembled normalcy. Knowing it belonged to a great great aunt who had traveled across America and into Canada, might make an impression. Besides, I would add that Winnipesaukee would want it that way.

The only thing I hadn't checked was a wooden box beside the bed where Winnipesaukee's body had laid so I decided to empty its contents, and then throw the box and whatever was combustible inside it, into the fire.

I opened the lid and reached inside. The first thing I drew out was a brown envelope, and on it was written, *My Last Will and Testament by Frank Lawdry*. The envelope itself had seen much better days. It was obviously old as the writing was faded and I had never seen any envelopes like it. There were stains on it from years gone by and it even smelled old.

I did hesitate for a moment because I didn't feel it was up to me to see this. However, this might have been what the old man said he wanted to give me. Besides, I must admit I was very curious. What did he even have to give to anyone? He owned no land and there was nothing of value in the contents of his house.

I turned it over and could see that it had been taped shut at one time but the tape was starting to peel off. I reached inside and pulled out one piece of paper. The paper was almost in as bad shape as the envelope. Winnipesaukee must have kept it on his kitchen table for years before deciding to put it in an envelope.

The handwriting was quite legible but the coal oil lamp didn't give off that much light from where I sat on the bed so I took it over to the table.

In very clear handwriting, Winnipesaukee had written his last will and testament. It was surprising how legible the writing was but then I remembered that the Lawdry family had been a privileged family in the east. Those few years of education showed through in his writing even though he was only thirteen when he lost his parents on the wagon trail.

I began reading it and as I read, I understood why Winnipesaukee wanted to give this to me. It would have been better to receive it in person. A few directions would have helped.

I, Frank Lawdry, being of sound mind and capable of making my own decisions, have written up my last will and testament.

I am leaving the only worldly possessions that are worth anything to the son that I have never seen since the day he was born. If he is not alive when I die, then it is to be left to any of his offspring.

The worldly goods that I have were received by dishonest means although the woman I took them from was not worthy of them either. Depending on my son's character, he may accept them or reject them. It will be entirely up to his conscience; however, time has passed by and I'm sure the memory of them by the original owner has been forgotten.

On the south side of the Qu'Appelle River under a large evergreen tree at the bottom of a high mound, you will find three gold nuggets buried. They are stored in a metal box and buried some two feet beneath the surface.

That is all I have to offer. Signed, Frank Lawdry

I folded the paper in four and put it in my jeans pocket. There was no point in handing this over to Toby. What was I to do? Keep it until he grew up and see if he wanted to hunt for the treasure?

The events of the day took their toll on me. I hardly had the strength to pick myself up off the bed. It must have been way past midnight by now. The fire was burning low and Rosie was settled into a corner near the back of the shed with easy access to hay if she so desired. I blew out the lamp and collapsed on the second bed. I could not bring myself to lie down where Winnipesaukee had just spent his last night.

During the night, I could hear the wind howling around the corners of the cabin and the low rumble of thunder off in the distance. When I awoke, the sky was gray and the air was cool.

My stomach was surely touching my backbone and I was not in the mood for a cup of boiled coffee even if I could find some. I needed to haul that old piano over to Lilly's house and trade it for a good breakfast.

Mostly everything in the shed was useless but I did find an old harness that must have been used for a team of horses years back. I was sure neither Sarah nor Frank ever owned a team but perhaps some of the Métis passing through had left it. Leaning against one wall was an old wooden skid that I figured Winnipesaukee had used for hauling barrels of water up from the river. Perhaps chopping a hole in the ice in winter and bringing up water. Anyway, this day, it would make do for hauling a piano.

Perhaps the most difficult dilemma I faced was moving that small piano out the door, although I figured that if Winnipesaukee could get it in, I should be able to get it out. Finally, after taking the legs off and putting it on its side, I was able to maneuver it out the door. I screwed the legs back on and then, as gently as I could, tipped it onto the skid. I was sure all of this moving and banging around would have a profound effect on the piano's performance but someone else could deal with that problem.

It wasn't the fanciest get-up and Rosie wasn't particularly pleased about pulling it but I walked beside her and held her bridle and that seemed to settle her down.

Toby was sitting out by the river waiting for us. His eyes grew huge when he saw what we were hauling.

"You brought us Sarah's piano?" he shouted.

I stopped Rosie so he could run over and check it out.

"You didn't burn it!" he said.

"Toby, I would never burn a piano. I'm not even finished going through all your grandfather's things. I thought your grandma might like this."

Lilly heard the commotion and came out.

"Oh my word!" she said, "I didn't know Frank Lawdry had a piano."

I nodded. "Well, even if you went inside, you could easily not see it. It was covered with piles of books, papers, and clothes. His sister, Sarah, loved to play. I'm not sure if she ever played this one though. I have a feeling he bought it after she died."

"Why on earth would someone do that?"

"Grandma, it's because he could look at it and think of her." He stared at his grandmother as if wondering how anyone could not understand that. "That's what we'll do too. We can look at that and think of Winnipesaukee."

She looked at me and rolled her eyes. "Lord, that's all I need - memories of that old man." She turned to the boy. "We aren't staying here forever, you know. Now we've found your grandfather and as soon as I'm better, and you get back from your trip with Patrick, we can go back home."

"I hope you don't mind my asking, Lilly, but why did you come here anyway? It seems a lot of trouble just to find some long lost relative."

She hesitated and then said, "Well, you might as well know. There was gossip in the family that the old man was in possession of some kind of treasure that he'd stolen from his wife before running away. I know it sounds crazy, but what did I have to lose? I figured to come up and see. Toby might be his only living relative."

"Did you ask the old man about it?"

"Are you kidding? I stood at the doorway once and that was enough for me. He was a crazy old hermit."

Toby glared at her. "He was not crazy."

"Well, he definitely wasn't what I'd expected. He was almost starving but he was too proud to take handouts. He was filthy dirty, and he wandered all over the place, scaring people half to death. That's pretty close to crazy, Toby."

Toby put his head down and I knew he was about to cry.

I turned to his grandmother. "You can do whatever you want with the piano. When you go back to your home, leave the piano in the house if you like. There is a favor I'd like to ask though."

"What is it? Please don't ask me to finish cleaning up that cabin. My heart couldn't take it."

I laughed. "No, I was wondering if you might have something to eat. I'm half starving. Winnipesaukee had nothing in the house to eat."

She nodded and gave me a knowing look. "See, I told you he was a crazy old coot."

"No, he wasn't," Toby cried. "He knew he was going to die; that's why he stopped eating."

"It seems that he told you that I was dying too but I'm still alive and it's a good thing too or you wouldn't have anything to eat."

That put an end to that conversation and we ate in silence.

Now I had a conundrum with which to deal. Should I read Winnipesaukee's Will to her? Everything in me said that the proper thing to do would be to give it to her. After all, Toby was probably Winnipesaukee's only living relative. That would be the proper thing to do but would it be the wisest? What would she do? Start digging under every tree at the bottom of a large mound? A person could probably spend a lifetime and not find that treasure - if it were even treasure. What if what he stole was not as valuable as he thought? What was worth something over sixty or seventy years ago might be worthless in today's market.

Lilly herself sealed the deal when she said, "Even if that old geezer was worth a million, I wouldn't want it."

Toby came back to the cabin with me. Lilly had packed a little knapsack for him with strict orders to obey every word that I said, and not to be a bother.

"And don't be talking all the time. You wear a body out with all that nonsense you talk," she said.

It sounded a bit harsh to me but I believe she had more feelings for the boy than she would have liked to admit.

"I should be coming back by fall, Miss Lilly," I said. "Mr. Pike is expecting me then and I have to return his horse."

"Well, Toby doesn't mind walking so I'm sure he can keep up with you."

"No, we'll ride double. Rosie won't mind and we can make better time."

We left for Winnipesaukee's cabin then, both of us walking. Rosie was happy not to be pulling that old piano. I left the skid and the harness in the dilapidated barn at the back of the house.

Lilly was kind enough to provide supplies to last for a day or two. She put a few of Toby's clothes in a small gunnysack along with a Bible. I imagine that was to remind him that he wasn't the pagan that he appeared to be.

Toby, I noticed, never once even glanced back at his grandmother as we started down the path. I looked back and Lilly was standing on the porch, watching us. I waved and she waved back.

On the way to the cabin, we stopped twice - once to stand for a few moments at Frank and Sarah's graves and another time to fill up on saskatoon berries again.

The cabin was now almost bare. Toby was quiet as we walked from one end to the other, checking under the beds and looking into drawers to see if there was anything else we should throw out and burn.

The picture of Sarah and Winnipesaukee with the Métis leader, Louis Riel, still hung on the wall.

"When we come back, Toby," I said, "take that picture and keep it."

"Why?"

"I know you aren't old enough to see the value in old pictures but it would make a good keepsake."

He shrugged. "I was hoping more for maybe some of Winnipesaukee's fishing hooks or something."

I grinned at him. "I saw some in the old shed. Let's hide them so no one can find them and then when you come back, you can retrieve them."

"Retrieve? What does that mean?"

"That means we'll find them and you can keep them. Does that sound better?"

He nodded.

I took down the picture and hid it along with several old fishhooks underneath one of the loose floorboards where the piano had stood.

We saddled up Rosie and started on our journey to see my pa. Toby sat behind me with his short arms wrapped around my waist.

Chapter Twenty

It was another hot dry day. Once again, there were signs of rain in the west but whether it would reach us was another question. As most days, it vanished into nothing. No one would believe it was real rain until he or she stood in it and got soaked to the bone. I tried to stick to the gravel highway but many times, we struck out across an empty field to try to cut off a few miles. Unfortunately, several times we came to either thick bush, cattle grazing on the other side of a barbed wire fence, or steep ravines, so we had to turn back to find the road again. All this took extra time.

The going was slow. Rosie seemed to plod along, perhaps brooding that she had two bodies to carry now, although one was a small one. I wasn't on the heavy side either. After Molly died, I lost my desire for food so I mostly ate because if I wanted to keep living, I had to eat. When there is no incentive to keep living, a person doesn't take much pleasure in food.

When we came to a body of water, we would take our overalls off and jump in. It not only washed our smelly bodies but cleaned our underwear too. When our food supply ran low, we would stop at a town and see what we could buy for the few pennies and nickels we had left. Or, we would raid someone's garden. A few times, the farmer or his wife caught us but when they heard our tale of woe, we usually ended up with a good meal and some food to take with us. One farmer gave us a fishing rod that he claimed he never used anymore and his wife found an old frying pan so we could cook up some fish along the way.

"The lakes are teeming with fish, son," he said. "No need to starve here in Saskatchewan."

The problem with moving along slowly, day after day, is that your mind starts to think the wrong kind of thoughts.

We'd camped in a pretty spot beside a small lake one night. As the farmer said, it was teeming with fish - some of the biggest Perch I'd ever seen. I still had a little grease the farmer's wife had given me in a pint sealer so after scraping off the scales as best I could and trying to debone it, I threw that fish in the hot frying pan. It sizzled and turned golden brown in minutes. In fact, it was so fresh, one piece jumped in the pan, sending Toby into a fit of laughter.

Yes, it should have been a night to bring joy to my heart. However, after bedding down under a deep-scented pine tree, my heart was anything but joyful. Perhaps, it was the fact that I had felt some joy and it made me feel guilty. Molly had given her life up for our child but now both were dead; how could I selfishly enjoy myself?

That pain stayed with me long into the night until I could not take it anymore. What right did I have to live? Molly's father was right. I, too, should be dead.

I crept out from under the pine branches and walked slowly to the lake. It was so many years ago, but the feeling has never left me. I knew what I had to do. First, I walked in until my feet were covered and I stood for a moment, looking up at the full moon. The air was still but the sweet scent of pine pressed against my skin. It was my burial cloak. I moved forward until the water reached my waist. A deep sense of relief filled me, as I knew it would soon be over. Soon, my hurt and pain would be washed away forever. Who was there to miss me? My own father never answered my letters. Did he even want me coming home? My sweet mother was gone and my sweet Molly was gone. I had nothing to live for. I stepped farther until the water was to my chest. I closed my eyes and thought how serene it all was. How easy it was going to be. How much better off everyone would be after I was gone.

"Patrick?"

A child's frightened voice filled the still night air.

All was silent.

"Patrick? What are you doing, Patrick?"

I turned slowly and looked at the small boy standing on the shore. In the moonlight, I could see the confusion in his eyes and see his body shaking with fright. He wrapped his arms across his chest to make the shaking stop. As I stood watching, I saw the tears roll down his cheeks. He did nothing to stop them.

"Toby," I said. "Why are you crying? Don't cry. I'm not going to leave you. Did you think I was going to swim across the lake?" I tried to laugh but it was harsh and foreign-sounding in my ears. "There's no need to cry. I couldn't sleep so I thought I would go for a swim. That's all. Go back to sleep now."

He stood staring at me for several seconds and then shook his head.

"No, I won't go to sleep until you do."

I cannot describe the shame that filled my soul. How could anyone be so selfish? Was I not thinking of the child who would wake up in the morning and find himself all alone? No, I wasn't. I was thinking only of myself and taking an easy way out.

That was the day Toby Lawdry saved my life.

Chapter Twenty one

Some leaves were starting to turn red and gold by the time we reached my father's homestead. It had been a long journey and I couldn't imagine going all the way back to Mr. Pike's farm - at least, not on horseback. In fact, my backside was telling me that it never wanted to sit in a saddle again!

I gently pulled the reins back and Rosie stood still. Somewhere in the distance, I heard a crow call out and another answer from farther away. The smell from wild roses along the ditch and a hint of dust from the sandy road filled the air. To my left, nestled in the bush, surrounded by poplar trees to the north, was the log house my father and grandfather had built. Nothing had changed in the few years I'd been away. I wasn't sure what time it was but it seemed strange that there was no smoke coming from the chimney. My stomach told me it was time for supper.

Toby moved to look around me. "Is this it, Patrick? Is this your Pa's house?"

I nodded. "This is it. Doesn't look like anyone's home though, does it?"

"Maybe we should just go in and see. I'd sure like to get something to eat."

I touched Rosie with my foot and she moved forward. She must have felt that we had reached our destination because she started trotting as we made our way up the road to the house. The road was starting to fill in with grass and as we got closer, I could see things were beginning to look rundown. Was my father not well? I wouldn't be surprised if my grandfather had died. After all, he was getting up in years. Mostly I think his antagonistic nature was what kept him going as long as it did.

I rode Rosie up close to the house and reached around for Toby. As I held him, he slipped slowly down to the ground.

"Looks like nobody lives here, Patrick," he said. "You sure this is your old house?"

I laughed. "Of course, I know this is my house, Toby. I haven't been gone that long."

After leading Rosie closer to the house and dropping her lines, I yelled out, "Anybody home? Pa, where are you? This is Patrick. I'm home."

We both stood silent. Toby's lips were in a straight line and his eyes were wide. The only sound was the wind whispering through the poplar trees behind the house and Rosie munching on some grass.

"Let's just go to the house, Toby. It's obvious my pa is out somewhere."

Tall grass and weeds covered the path to the door. This was when I became a bit anxious. What had happened? Where was my father?

The old wooden door creaked and groaned as I pushed it open. The kitchen was as I remembered it except it smelled like the inside of a dusty gunnysack. No one had opened a window in a long time. There was a layer of fine dust on everything.

Without saying anything, we walked from the kitchen into the small living room. All the furniture sat just as it always had. Nothing was out of place. On the floor, by the iron potbellied stove, there was a stack of cut wood. My mother's embroidered pillow was nestled in the corner of the sofa and the old wooden rocking chair that had been my grandmother's still stood in its place.

The door off the living room led to my parent's bedroom. The first thought that came to me was that my father might be lying in that bed, dead, like Winnipesaukee.

"Stay here, Toby," I ordered, as I walked over to the door.

A bed with a wrought-iron headboard almost filled the room. In one corner at the foot of the bed was a chest of drawers and on the wall were several wooden hooks for hanging clothes. My father's overalls were on one hook and there was nothing on the other three.

My grandmother's quilt covered the bed the same as it had for as long as I could remember.

There was no dead body.

Where was my father?

I wasn't thinking about Toby. My mind was on finding out what happened to my pa. Toby followed behind me as I went into the second bedroom off the kitchen. This had been my grandparent's bedroom and then, after Grandma died, my grandfather said I could leave my narrow sleeping area in the attic and share his bed but I declined the offer. It was bad enough listening to Grandpa's snoring from up above the living room. Sometimes it was a nuisance bringing in the ladder and climbing up through the opening but I appreciated that bit of privacy. Usually that was the only privacy I ever enjoyed.

I stopped in the doorway and glanced around the room. The quilt on the bed was pushed back as if my grandfather had lifted it up so he could fling his legs over the side. I doubt he had ever made up a bed in his lifetime. His gray flannel shirt and worn denim overalls hung on the pegs on the wall, at the end of the bed. The flowered wallpaper was starting to peel and the curtains on the one and only window were as dirty as the windowpane itself. The room smelled stuffy and I had no desire to enter.

The only place I knew to look next was the small graveyard back in the woods behind the house. Surely, if my father and grandfather both died, someone would have notified me. Perhaps, someone had tried and I hadn't received the information? But there was no reason why my father wouldn't have sent word if Grandpa had passed away.

The path to the graveyard was almost indiscernible and even walking through the tall grass was not easy. I spotted the low white picket fence almost completely hidden by the growth. My heart sank. If my father were here, he would have never let this happen. In fact, he took great pride in having his family buried so close by. Oftentimes, I would see him walk out, pulling weeds as he went, and stand looking down at the graves. I believe my father carried guilt in his heart the same way I carried it in mine. My mother was a soft gentle woman, a lovely person who would have preferred spending her days reading or perhaps sitting out by a river, listening to the murmuring water. Instead, she labored day and night, trying to keep up with the upkeep of a farmhouse. Many times, especially when Pa was busy in the fields, she would don my father's overalls to clean out the chicken coop and the barn.

"What is this place?"

I whirled around. Toby stood behind me. How could I have forgotten him?

"This is a graveyard."

He came up beside me. "Who's dead here?"

"My grandmother, my mother, and my brother."

"Where's your pa?"

I sighed. "That's what I came out to see, Toby."

"Is he here?"

I shrugged. "I don't know. It doesn't look like it but I'm going to walk around to see."

"Can I come?"

"If you like."

The gate was so overgrown with weeds that I had to throw my leg over the fence, and then pick Toby up and lift him over.

I checked around the area where I knew my father had buried his mother, his wife, and his son, but that was all I could see. If anyone had died lately, there was no sign of a freshly dug grave.

"Where you think they've gone, Patrick?"

I shook my head. "I wish I knew, Toby."

With a solemn look and eyes opened wide, he said, "I think they're dead."

It was difficult suppressing a grin.

"Not everyone dies, Toby."

"Then where are they?" He stared at me. "Everyone who knows you or me, dies."

"Don't think like that. It's depressing."

"What does that mean? Depressing?"

"It means sad. When you talk like that, it makes people sad. It even makes you sad."

It appeared he had to think about that for a while, so as he was mulling it over in his mind, I was also mulling something. How could two men disappear? Surely, if they had been sick and died, someone would have known to bury them in the graveyard behind the house. I walked over and checked again. There were no fresh graves. Tall weeds, almost to my waist, covered the whole area.

I looked over at Toby.

"I know what we'll do first, Toby."

"Clean up the graveyard?"

"No, we'll go to the house and make something to eat. You can pump some water for Rosie and settle her in the barn."

"We're not going to look for your Pa?"

I shook my head. "Not today. We'll get up early and ride over to the neighbor's. I'm sure they'll know what's going on."

He nodded. "I'm sure they will, Patrick. Maybe they're even buried somewhere else. Maybe the neighbors buried them."

"Toby, I think we've talked enough about death and graveyards. Let's see if we can't find something to eat and then have a good sleep. You can sleep in my grandpa's bed."

His eyes widened. "You don't think he'll mind. I ain't smelling very good."

I laughed. "I think it will be okay. Grandpa didn't always smell too fresh either. Tomorrow, we can bring out the galvanized tin tub from the shed and have a bath before we go to the neighbor's."

So the two of us settled down to a meal of biscuits made with flour, water, and a bit of salt, and a jar of canned tomatoes that I found in the cold room out in one of the sheds. I wasn't sure how old it was but there were quite a few quarts of tomatoes so I imagine the two men just didn't fancy them. I can't say I did too much either but it filled our bellies.

152

"You figuring on giving me some coffee too?" Toby asked.

"I think you're too young for coffee. My mother didn't let me drink coffee until I was sixteen."

"That's all you were feeding me at Winnipesaukee's."

I couldn't hide my grin. "I guess you're right. You've been as good a helper as any man so I guess you deserve a cup of coffee."

It was good to see Toby finally smile.

Even filled with all that caffeine, the boy was almost asleep before I left the room. It's true, he wasn't smelling as clean as he could but the sheets didn't appear to be as clean as they could either.

After I'd tucked him in, I cleaned up the kitchen, and then walked outside. It was a beautiful night with another bright moon shining down, casting deep shadows across the yard. What was I doing up here in the bush, far away from everyone, with a small boy whom I didn't even know? And where were my father and grandfather? Folks don't disappear like that. There was no clue as to where they went. Didn't they think I might come home some day?

My last thoughts before I went back inside were of Molly. They were always of Molly at night. In all the struggles going on in my mind, Molly was the only memory that made any sense to me.

Chapter Twenty Two

We didn't get the early start that next morning that I'd been hoping for. It seemed the long journey with all its hardships had taken its toll. The stress of finally reaching our destination only to find no one at home had left a deep empty feeling inside me. It was late morning when I finally opened my eyes. I looked around and for a moment, wondered where I was. Not until I saw my father's overalls on the peg did I remember.

The house was still except for a fly buzzing and hitting itself repeatedly against the windowpane. My mind strayed back to my childhood. The silent house after my mother died. My grandfather would be doing the chores while my father stood in the pasture, staring out at nothing. I felt alone now until I remembered that I was not the only person in the house. When I did, I jumped out of bed and ran to the other bedroom. To my relief, Toby was asleep.

I slowly closed his bedroom door so as not to waken him and tried to think of what I could make for breakfast. We always had chickens so our breakfasts consisted of three or four eggs each with a thick slice of ham, but there were no hens scratching and pecking freely around the yard and no pigs rolling in the mud beside the barn. In fact, it was eerily quiet - no dogs barking, no cows bawling to be milked, and not even a cat sitting by the barn waiting for her first taste of warm milk. These were all the sounds that I associated with my home.

Perhaps if I went outside and walked about, I might solve this mystery. Or, at least, find some clue as to my father's whereabouts. I had a hankering to do it anyway. The walls were starting to press in on me.

It was turning out to be, as usual, another warm day but already there was a touch of coolness to the breeze. It was no longer just hot air hitting your skin. I was thinking it must be about the middle of August. What a terrible thing that I, not only never knew the time of day, I didn't even know what month it was or the day of the week. What was I planning to do with my life anyway? I needed someone to take me by the hand and lead me. Or, so it seemed.

I heard Rosie whinnying from inside the barn so I led her out and removed the rope from her halter. She shook her head as if she'd been freed from a prison and trotted a few feet in front of me before stopping to bend her head and eat. The tall grass almost touched her underbelly so I knew she would never stray. The dugout wasn't too far away so I went in that direction. I was curious to see if there was any water left in it after all the years without rain. I was still within yelling distance from Toby in case he woke up and ventured outside, worried as to where I went.

I was standing at the edge of the dugout, staring down into the large empty abyss when I heard him call.

"I'm here, Toby," I yelled back. "Stay there."

There was no point looking at the empty dugout any longer. How could every living thing have disappeared within the past year or so? Was there no sign of life anywhere? Obviously, my father had decided to pack up and leave. Had he left everything in the house in case I returned? Would he be returning soon too?

I dragged my feet back to the house. My one consolation was the fact Toby and I had a roof over our heads for the next few days anyway. Perhaps the only option I had was to return the boy to his grandmother and I would continue on my way back to the Pike farm. For some reason, my father and grandfather had left so suddenly they never even took their overalls from off their pegs.

For breakfast, I made biscuits with flour, water, and baking soda. I was pleased to find the can of baking soda but the results showed that it wasn't too potent anymore. They were flat but still tasted good. There was an unopened jar of homemade blueberry jam in the back of a shelf in the cupboard so we felt as if we'd dined like kings. The jam reminded me of all the work my mother used to do and I wondered if the men folk ever appreciated it as much as they should have.

"What are we going to do now?" Toby asked, as he wiped some jam off his chin with his sleeve. "You know, seeing as everyone's died. Will we have to go back to my grandmother's house now? She might be dead now too, you know."

"First of all, Toby, we don't know what happened. Once we find out, we can figure out what to do. I'm sure your grandmother is doing fine. I don't want you worrying about it."

He shrugged. "I ain't worrying."

"Ain't isn't a word."

He stared at me. "Course it is. I just said it."

"I mean it isn't good English. You should say 'I'm not' instead."

"Who told you that?"

"My mother."

We sat in the living room and drank our coffee. I felt guilty but I had no milk to give the boy.

When we finished, I said, "Let's walk round my father's farm and see what we can find out."

"Okay. Do you think we'll find their bodies? Maybe they had an accident and nobody's found them."

There was no point arguing with a boy set on having everyone dead so I just agreed.

I shrugged. "Could be, Toby. Why don't we go and check it out."

We retraced my steps back towards the dugout. Dark billowing clouds were now bubbling up in the east and the sun was slowly disappearing behind them.

"Let's not dally," I said. "We don't want to be too far away when it starts to rain."

For the next fifteen minutes, we walked around the dugout and a ways into the meadow. The meadow was where the cattle and our team of horses spent their days when they weren't hard at work. It too was overgrown with tall grass and clover. Bees hovered above the clover as if there was such a variety they didn't know which flower to settle down on. Across the meadow, there was a bluff of poplars and spruce. Songs of various birds filled the air. Somewhere in the distance, we heard thunder rumbling.

"Maybe we'd better head back, Patrick." The temperature had cooled down quickly and the breeze had turned into a wind.

"I think you're right," I said. By the time we reached the house, the rain was descending in sheets.

"What about Rosie?" he yelled.

"Don't worry about that old nag; she can take care of herself."

He probably didn't hear me as the wind came up so quickly we had to race the last few steps, holding our shirts over our heads. As it was, we were both soaked. We took off our shirts off and hung them over the kitchen chairs.

Even inside the house, the air was beginning to smell fresher.

I parted the kitchen curtains to look out into the yard and sure enough, Rosie was already inside her barn, looking out. She was enjoying the miracle of rain as much as we were.

Rain poured down from the heavens for the rest of the morning. Within an hour, the weeds were taking on a fresh green hue. Toby was content sitting at the window and watching the rain.

"Do you think the whole earth is going to be flooded?" he asked.

"Goodness, no. Why are you asking that? This is just a late summer storm."

He bent over and gazed up. "I don't think it's going to stop. Grandma says there was a flood all over the earth a long time ago. Maybe it's happening again."

"Well, my grandma said it would never happen again."

"How did she know?"

"God said."

"Oh."

To fill in my time, I decided to look through the drawers in my father's desk, the only piece of furniture that was worth anything. If I remembered correctly, my parents found it alongside the road as they traveled north to their new homestead in Saskatchewan. My mother polished it until the old scratched-up wood shone.

Now the drawers stuck so it took a few pushes and pulls for them to scrape open. There were four drawers and each was filled with my father's important papers. As I sorted through them, they didn't appear to be of any particular interest to me. In the second drawer, however, under a pile of bills marked 'paid in full', there was a stack of letters held together with a rubber band. I stared down at the first one.

This was an unopened letter addressed to me. By the date that the post office had stamped on the envelope, it was when I was just about to marry Molly. Written beside the address, which I knew was my father's writing, someone had scratched in pencil, 'Wrong address. No one here by that name.'

I picked the letter up and under it were three more letters, all of them unopened, and all returned to my father.

I recognized the handwriting on the envelope.
Jacob Jordan.

Molly's father had returned all of my father's letters. No wonder I thought my father had forgotten me. Then, it came to me - I had never personally mailed a letter to my father. Mr. Jordan always took the mail to town to send it out. Had my father received any of *my* letters? Or had Mr. Jordan ripped them up and thrown them away? A feeling of rage and dread filled me as I realized what a wicked man Molly's father truly was. How could he have hated me so much? Even before my Molly died, he hated me.

Chapter Twenty Three

I opened each letter and read it.

My father wasn't much of letter writer. He was a boy when they came to Canada and instead of going to school, he helped his father on the farm. My grandmother taught him as best she could but all they knew was hard work and schooling didn't seem that important.

The letters were all much the same. He wondered why they hadn't heard from me. He supposed I was too busy to write. There was always a paragraph about the weather and the crops. Neither were encouraging. In each letter he wondered why his previous letter had come back unopened.

I held back my tears for Toby's sake. I looked over at him. He had moved from the window and now sat on the old sofa, staring up at the ceiling.

"Toby, why don't you go outside and play for awhile? The storm is over and the sun is out. I'll finish going through these drawers and then we'll visit the neighbors." I forced a smile. "If the old buggy is still round back somewhere, maybe we could hitch Rosie up and take that. What do you think?"

It was the first time he had smiled all morning.

"That would be fun." He slid off the sofa. "Maybe I'll go out and see if I can find it. I should check on Rosie too."

I watched as he walked out. He was a little boy who should be playing outside. I had played all by myself, climbing trees, building forts, having pretend battles, but it seemed Toby didn't know how. He was too old for his age.

I turned back to my job of cleaning out my father's desk drawers. No one had entered the house after my father and grandfather left; or if they had, nothing had been disturbed. Could the two be on their way to southern Saskatchewan to visit me? Were they worried something happened to me because all the letters came back? They must have been concerned; otherwise, if my father hadn't cared, he would have thrown those old letters away a long time ago. Or, could he be angry with me, thinking that I'd given him a wrong address or that I was not where I was supposed to be? So many perplexing questions raced through my brain.

The rest of the drawers were filled with receipts from bills paid. My father had always been conscientious about that. You would never try to charge my father twice for anything if he'd already paid for it.

The dates on the bills were what interested me the most. What was the most current one? That could tell me how long my father had been gone.

In the bottom of one drawer, I found a long narrow ledger. I stared down at the last item my father had recorded. It was dated a year before. I flipped through the next pages in case he'd missed a few by mistake, but no, there it was - a little over one year ago, my father had made his last entry. Where had my father been for the past year? If he'd travelled down to look for me riding horseback or even walking, it wouldn't have taken this long.

Chapter Twenty Four

There were two sheds behind the house and a small barn built close to the woods on the north side. My mother insisted on having it a ways from the house. I suspect she hoped the manure would rub off onto the ground before my father arrived at the back door. My grandfather thought it should be attached to the house but when my father saw the look of horror on Mother's face, he vetoed that idea.

"I found it!" Toby stood inside the back door. His eyes were bright and he was grinning, showing all his teeth. It was the most emotion I'd seen on the kid since I'd met him.

"Found what?"

"The buggy. It's small enough for one horse to pull. I think Rosie will love it."

I smiled at him. No one ever thinks of a horse loving anything but oats.

"That's wonderful, Toby." I glanced down at the papers I'd scattered all over the desk and sofa. "I can't do much else here so I'll leave it for now. Let's hitch Rosie up."

It appeared that Toby was right. Rosie might love her oats but it also seemed that she loved pulling a buggy. The grin on Toby's face stayed there all the way to the neighbor's yard.

All the years we had homesteaded, Alvin Becker and his wife, Esther, had lived two miles down the road. They had no children and I believe they were both misanthropists. Most of the time, no one even knew they existed. As a child, I couldn't help but feel uneasy whenever we went to their place. It wasn't that we were ever invited but sometimes you do require a neighbor for a specific need. Mr. Becker would often lend my father the use of some farm equipment but I always felt he did it in a begrudging way. Esther would stand on the step watching every move I made so I mostly stood very still. Folks in the area stayed away from them and that suited them just fine. These were our closest neighbors though and if anything had happened to my father and grandfather, they were the ones who would hopefully know.

It was a pleasant ride to their homestead. The buggy creaked and swayed with each bump on the sandy road. The sand, already dry after all that rain, muffled the sound of Rosie's hooves as the dust drifted up in front of the buggy. Nothing had changed while I'd been gone. The road was just wide enough for one vehicle. If that vehicle happened to be a car, truck, or tractor, the buggy moved into the ditch. If it were two vehicles meeting, they tried either sharing the road or one was kind enough to pull over into the ditch and wait for the other to pass. That, of course, usually entailed a lengthy visit, each lauding the superior performance of their vehicle.

I looked over at the little boy beside me. As I watched him staring off at the trees, I realized that he was probably bored.

"Here, Toby," I said. "Why don't you hold the reins?"

It was as if I had turned on a light switch. His grin stretched from one side of his face clear to the other side.

He was still grinning when we approached the gate into the Becker's yard.

"Here's where we turn, Toby. Rosie only knows to neck rein so hold the reins over to the right so she'll feel them on her neck."

The horse responded and turned onto the trail leading to the house. The Beckers had no gate but they did have poles placed over the ditch so no stray cattle would cross. Rosie didn't hesitate and the buggy bounced over the logs making so much noise I'm sure the homeowners could hear our approach. The house itself was in a clearing about half a mile through the bush. As autumn approached, the leaves would drop and passersby on the road would be able to see the buildings from the road. Now, no one would even be aware of anyone living there. Grass grew up down the center of the narrow road and scratched along the underside of the buggy. The cool darkness, however, was a pleasing break from the hot sun. Tree branches brushed against the buggy and occasionally one would smack us in the face, sending Toby into a fit of laughter.

As we left the shade of the driveway, it took a few seconds for our eyes to adjust to the bright sunlight again.

Alvin Becker must have heard the buggy crossing over the poles because he stood on the step, arms crossed against his chest. He wore denim overalls, worn and dirty. An old straw hat hung over his face almost touching his nose. White whiskers covered his chin and the sides of his face.

As soon as I saw him look up, I waved and called out, "Hello, Mr. Becker." I took over the reins from Toby as I pulled the buggy closer to the house. "I reckon you remember me - Patrick Smithson. How are you and the missus?"

He lifted his hat off his face and settled it on the back of his head. He didn't utter a word. I felt Toby moving closer to me.

"It's okay, Toby. This here is our neighbor, Mr. Becker. He's the one who might know where my pa and grandpa are." I looked back to the man standing on the steps. "You happen to know what's happened to them, sir?"

"Can't say I do." He moved a chunk of chewing tobacco to the other cheek and sent a spew of spit through the air.

If he's been any closer, the gob would have smacked Rosie on her belly.

"When was the last time you saw them, sir, if you don't mind me asking?"

He shrugged. "Maybe a year or so ago."

"A year? Really? Didn't you wonder where they were?"

"None of my business." He spit again. "Just like what I do is none of theirs."

"But surely you ran into them on the road or maybe in town."

"Nope. I never ran into them."

"You didn't hear anything? Like when they were threshing? Sound travels real far out here in the country. Surely you heard that."

"Can't say I did. Nope. I didn't hear anything."

"But if you didn't, weren't you concerned?"

"I told you - it weren't none of my concern."

I saw a movement in the window and saw Mrs. Becker with her face up to the pane, staring at us.

"So you have no information about them at all. No one talked about them at the store?"

He shook his head. "I don't know anything about your pa. How many times do I have to tell you? Last I saw your grandpa, he was chasing a moose that was heading onto my field, and I told him if he shot it on my land, I'd shoot him."

"You said you'd shoot my grandpa?"

"Not that I'd do it but I don't appreciate anyone coming onto my land."

"When was that? Do you recall?"

He shrugged. "Maybe a year or so ago."

"That was maybe a year ago and that's the last time you saw my grandpa?"

"I ain't gonna stand here all day and keep telling you this." He shook his head and started to turn back into the house.

I could see that I was getting nowhere with this man and I was mostly frustrating myself, so I picked up the reins, preparing to leave.

"There was the time that man came, Alvin."

Mrs. Becker suddenly appeared beside her husband.

"Yeah, but that ain't his pa or grandpa."

"What man was that, Mrs. Becker?" I asked.

"There was a man came asking where your pa lived. Seems he thought our place might be yours." Mrs. Becker moved closer to the edge of the veranda.

"When was that?"

She thought for a few seconds. "Must be about a year ago now." She looked back at her husband who had edged closer to the screen door. "Don't you think, Alvin?"

Mr. Becker shrugged again. "I don't keep track of all the folks who stop by here."

"Do you know what he wanted? Did he say anything at all about my father?"

Mrs. Becker shook her head. "I was listening from inside but he didn't seem like a very good man. He was using some language that wasn't fitting."

"Course, he was using that language. How'd he know you was inside?" Alvin glared at his wife. "That's how men talk when they're alone."

"Well, that don't make it right." She turned and looked at Toby. "The Lord can still hear it."

Mr. Becker spoke up. "That's about all we got, Smithson. We got no idea where your pa went to. Maybe he pulled out and moved away. He'd be a smart man if he did. This land here is killing us. And your pa was not much of a farmer to begin with. Seems those English folks are a bit too soft for this life."

I shook my head but not in disbelief. I already knew what Mr. Becker thought about people from England trying to be farmers. I wasn't going to argue with him because in some ways, I agreed. It seemed that it always took my grandfather and father twice the time to take off their crops or to do anything else on the farm.

"No, he didn't move away," I said. "The house is just as he left it. Nothing's been removed." I turned to his wife. "Do you remember how the man got here? Was he riding a horse or driving a car?"

"Oh, yes, I remember that. It ain't many who come into our yard driving a car. It was a nice one too, wasn't it, Alvin?"

All Mr. Becker seemed to do was shrug. "It was a Ford. Nothing special."

"Did the man say where he was from? Did he give you any information as to why he needed to see my father?"

They both shook their heads in unison.

170

Esther said, "And that seemed a bit strange too. You'd think if he came a ways, he might tell us why he was wanting your pa. It'd be polite to do that but he never said a word - just asked how to find your pa's place and then cussed when he found out this wasn't the right place. That's all."

"Can you remember what he looked like? Was he young or old?"

Mr. Becker kept quiet and let his wife do the rest of the talking.

"Hard to say. With all the troubles we're having with the drought and such, even young ones look old. Except for you, Mr. Smithson, you're still looking as young as can be. You must be having a good life."

"I'll be going on to twenty soon, ma'am. I ought to look young still."

I didn't tell her that inside of me, I felt like an old man because of all the trouble and pain that I'd been through.

She smiled and I realized that Esther Becker might have been a fine looking woman in years past. Now her skin looked like brown leather from working all day in the sun and I noticed a few teeth were missing. She was right when she said young ones were looking old but old ones looked ready for the grave before their time.

"Yes, I guess you are still young, Patrick. Well, I hope you can figure out where your Pa has gone. I wonder if that stranger ever did find him. We're leery of any strangers so we didn't want to ask any questions. To be honest, we were relieved when he drove away."

"Why's that?"

"I don't know. Just something about him. Alvin felt it too. He made us nervous."

"Can you describe him at all?"

She looked down at the ground, deep in thought.

"Well, I know his hair was long and greasy looking. His clothes were dirty and tattered and he had a big rifle lying on the top of the car seat, against the rear window."

"Was this a sedan or a coupe?"

She looked to her husband. "What does he mean?"

"He means did the car have a front and back seat or was there just the one seat."

"Oh." She looked back at me. "There was just the one seat. It wasn't a big car. It was black."

I was surprised how much information eventually came out of the two.

"You remember what his voice sounded like?"

They both stared at me.

"It sounded like a man's voice," she said.

"Nothing special then. He didn't have an accent?"

They both shook their heads.

I smiled. "Thanks to both of you. I appreciate your help."

As if noticing Toby to be a real person for the first time, Mrs. Becker said, "And who is this? Some of your kin?"

I shook my head. "No, this is a friend. I knew his great *great* grandfather. This is a summer trip for him before he goes back to school in the fall."

They both nodded, and without another word, turned and walked back into the house.

172

I turned the buggy around and handed the reins to Toby. If I hadn't needed that horse to take me back to Mr. Pike's, I would have gladly given her to that little boy.

All the way back to the farm, I couldn't get my mind off this man who was searching for my father. Who could he be? And why? Why would he be wanting to talk to my pa?

Chapter Twenty Five

I managed to scrounge up a few things to eat. None of which, looked or tasted anything close to delicious. We couldn't live on baking soda biscuits, canned tomatoes, and cooked dandelion leaves. Besides, the flour was running low. I didn't tell Toby I'd had to remove a few bugs from it. Although that probably wouldn't have bothered him in the least.

"There's a train siding about five miles up the other way, Toby, and sometimes the fellow there keeps a few supplies. This afternoon, I think we'll have to get over there and see if he's got any food to sell."

Toby's eyes lit up. "You mean taking Rosie and the buggy?"

I nodded. "We'll need the buggy if we have to bring supplies back."

174

The road leading north continued on the same as the one leading south to the Becker's farm. It was narrow and sandy. Tall grass filled the ditches and the thick forest of pine, spruce, and poplar grew right up to the ditch on either side of the road. How homesteaders thought they could cut through that forest and create farmland seemed like an impossible dream to me.

The earlier clouds had drifted away and now the sun beat down on us again. The air was fresh and smelled of pine. It was something that I did miss when I was in the south. The only odor I recalled from there was the constant smell of dust.

I was thinking about the south and about Molly when Toby brought me back to reality.

"Look, Patrick. Here comes a car."

He was right. It was in our path and didn't seem to be slowing down at all. Dust billowed out behind it, drifting into the woods with the breeze. I grabbed the reins, moved Rosie off into the ditch, and waited for the car to drive past. Instead, the motor car screeched to a stop beside us. Rosie shied but after a few calming words from Toby, she settled down.

"Say, there," the driver called out, over the sound of the motor and through the dust. "You're Patrick, aren't you?"

"Yes, sir. I can't say I recognize you though," I said.

He laughed. "Guess that's cause I used to sport a beard."

"Mr. Yake?"

He nodded. "Yep, that's me. Think I'll grow that beard back before winter comes though." He laughed again. "You bring your pa home with you?"

"Bring my pa home? No, I've been looking for my father. You don't know where he is either?"

A strange look came over his face. "That's odd. Everyone here thought he and your grandfather were down in the south with you."

I shook my head. "Not with me. In fact, I haven't heard from him or my grandfather in over a year. That's one of the reasons, I came back."

Mr. Yake didn't speak for a few seconds. He lifted his cap and ran his hand over his hair before putting it back on.

"That is strange. That fellow who came from there said your father and grandfather were both going down to stay with you for a while. I thought it was a bit odd. He didn't look like the type your pa would be associating with."

"Was he dirty looking with long hair?"

"That's right. You know who he is then?"

I shook my head. "No. Mrs. Becker described a man who stopped at their place, looking for our farm. Sounds like the same man. You didn't get a name, did you?"

He shook his head. "No, he mostly mumbled and when I asked when your dad would be back, he just shrugged and said, 'not for awhile.'"

"Where'd you see this fellow anyway?"

"I was delivering something to someone down the road and almost collided with him at your gate. The idiot pulled out onto the road without even looking."

"Mr. Yake, this doesn't sound good at all. I don't know what's going on but I have to find my pa. He couldn't simply disappear off the face of the earth. I don't know who this man was but something sounds terribly wrong. I'm thinking I should contact the RCMP. What do you think?"

"Well, I understand how you must feel, Patrick, but since this was over a year ago, I don't know what they can do. Maybe you and I can see what we can dig up first. If we involve the RCMP, they've got to come down from Prince Albert and I don't think they would be too interested in checking into the little bit of information we have. Where are you off to now?"

"Actually, we were heading to your place to see if you had any supplies. Toby and I have run out of food."

"I have some with me now that I can give you. Not much but enough for a few days. More, if you stretch it."

I'd always liked Henry Yake. He was a large jolly man. Oftentimes, a bit rough around the edges but an honest man. My father trusted him so I did too.

"Thanks, I appreciate that. Will five dollars be enough?"

"Don't worry about that, Patrick. You've got enough on your mind. We'll square up another day. "

The car lifted slightly as the heavy man exited. He opened the back door and grabbed a gunnysack, bulging with food.

"Mr. Yake, I can't take all that. Someone must be waiting for it."

He winked. "Never mind, young man, the folks who wanted this, have plenty to live on. And you call me Henry now. You aren't the young lad you used to be." He turned to Toby, "So, you must be Mr. Smithson's driver. I noticed that horse listens to every word you tell it."

Toby nodded. "She does listen to me. I ain't Patrick's driver though; I'm his friend."

"Well, are you now? And what's your name?"

"My name's Toby Lawdry. You think you could help us find Patrick's pa?"

"I surely will help and we'll find him, that's for sure."

In a softer voice, he turned to Patrick and said, "Why don't I stop off on my way back, and we'll do a search of your land? Or, at least as much as we can cover in an hour or so. What do you think?"

I stared at him. "You think we might find them somewhere buried on the land?"

"I hope not but let's check it out. Something doesn't sit right with me either. I didn't like that fellow and now I'm getting worried."

I nodded. "Me, too. I'll see you back at the house."

Toby turned Rosie around and we started back home, eating some of the dust from Mr. Yake's car.

Chapter Twenty Six

It was almost six by the time Henry Yake arrived at the farm. Toby and I had filled up on what my mother used to call a 'fry-up' except we were missing the sausages. The fried potatoes, onions, and carrots all tasted wonderful though. I was pleased to find a jar of bacon grease in the sack and it gave it a wonderful flavor. I think the old cast iron frying pan had enough grease burnt into it that it would give flavor to almost anything.

As soon as we heard the vehicle drive up, Toby and I went out the door to meet him. To our surprise, Henry opened the passenger door and out clamored his old hunting dog . It seemed he'd been an old dog when I left home but he hadn't changed much - only accumulated more weight as his master had. The first thing he did was waddle over to Toby, tail wagging, and sniffing him out.

"Brought old Tom with me, Patrick. That old hound can sniff out anything. You got something around with your pa's scent on it?"

I ran back inside and brought out Pa's old overalls that had been hanging on the peg.

Henry shoved them up against Tom's nose several times until he was sure the dog remembered the scent; then he said, "Go find him, Tom."

The old dog waddled around the yard, sniffing the grass and urinating on anything else he ran into. I didn't want to discourage Mr. Yake, but I had serious doubts about Tom finding anything. By the time, he finished the yard, I was sure he'd be too worn out to go any farther.

Tom proved me wrong. He took off in the direction of the dugout and we followed, Henry shouting encouragement to him, as we walked.

The old dog seemed to wander around the empty dugout for quite some time and I was getting anxious to get back to the house.

Toby, of course, was enjoying every minute of it.

When Tom stopped and appeared to be giving up, Henry shoved the overalls back against his nose again.

I'm not sure if the scent was drifting in the breeze or what but all of a sudden the dog headed for the thick woods. We followed but the brush was so thick that by the time we worked our way through to a small clearing, the dog was out of sight.

"Now what, Mr. Yake?" I asked.

Henry Yake laughed. "Now we wait for Tom to let us know where he is."

It didn't take long and we heard a mournful howl. We followed the sound and came to Tom, sitting beside a large pine.

In front of him was a pile of scattered bones.

Chapter Twenty Seven

I'll say the next few days are hard to recall. I was forever grateful to Henry Yake, as he knew exactly what we had to do. He was about the only one in the area who had a telephone so he contacted the Royal Canadian Mounted Police. It took them over two hours to arrive so in the meantime, I had to come to grips with the fact that my father and grandfather had met with a horrendous demise. Had the man with greasy long hair murdered them? And if so, why? It couldn't be that he came to rob them because there was nothing to steal. Besides, why would he specifically choose my father's farm?

Constable Mike Brady was the first officer that I talked to. I immediately felt at ease with him and as I talked, he listened, nodded, and smiled encouragingly. He was a patient person and listened intently as I told my story - not that there was much to tell. As I talked, a younger officer sitting on a chair by the window had his head bent, making notes in a small black notebook.

After we came back to the house with Henry, I could not bring myself to go back into those woods. I certainly wouldn't have taken Toby there again. Besides, they looked like human remains but on the other hand, we were not familiar with bones so it might have been bones from a large animal. Henry, of course, trusted Tom's scenting instincts but it made me feel better when he said the dog could have been mistaken. In our hearts, we knew the dog was right.

Toby and I stood outside on the back step when the two officers brought the bones out from the woods. They had carefully wrapped everything in cloth and I knew they were treating them as if they were two dead bodies.

"We'll have to check to make sure these are human remains, Patrick. If they are, we might be able to find out from them how the men died. Try not to think of the worst scenario if you can. When we have some news, I'll phone Mr. Yake and he can let you know that we're coming down." He smiled and shook my hand.

A question was dwelling on my mind so I had to ask, "Sir, do you think that perhaps they could have been in the woods hunting and were overtaken by wolves? Or maybe it was a hunting accident?"

"We checked for that first of all; however, there was no sign of a rifle. Also, it appears that someone may have buried them in a shallow grave but they were probably dug up by animals." He reached over and put his hand on my shoulder. "Try not to think too much about it. It will only upset you more. This is only our preliminary findings. We still haven't proven anything."

He was almost to the vehicle when he turned and came back. "Do you know if your father or grandfather were ever in any kind of accident? Did either of them ever break an arm or leg or anything like that?"

I tried to think back. It seemed one of them was always getting hurt on something.

"There was a hunting accident a few years back. I was only about ten or eleven but I remember my dad bringing my grandfather home in the back of the wagon. I guess I remember because there was so much blood in the wagon. It seems my grandfather tripped and the gun went off and shot him in the foot." I looked at him. "I don't know if that is any help to you."

He smiled. "That's exactly what I wanted to know. I'm sure it will be helpful, Patrick." He reached over and ruffled Toby's hair. "And you, young man, you look after Mr. Smithson here, all right?"

Toby, who, from the moment they arrived, had been mesmerized by the bright red uniforms and the shiny vehicle, gazed up at the officer in wonder, and nodded.

After the door shut, Toby announced, "That's what I want to be when I grow up. An RCMP officer."

Chapter Twenty Eight

For more than a week, the RCMP trampled through the woods. Toby and I stuck close to the house and often times took Rosie out so we could get away from it all. If my mind had not been on the small boy, the situation would have been much more traumatizing. As it was, I dreamt almost every night about the stranger chasing my elderly grandfather and just before the shot rang out, I would sit up in bed in a cold sweat. By morning, I felt exhausted.

Vehicles came and went. Reporters would try to come to the house but the officers would quickly send them back. Since I had no access to any newspapers and my father's radio hadn't worked for years, I had no idea what people were saying or thinking. Oftentimes, car groups would stop on the road and watch the house. I was sure it was the talk of all northern Saskatchewan.

At the end of the second week, a black unmarked car drove into the yard and a man in a black suit with a white shirt and red tie walked to the house. Even without the uniform, there was no mistaking that he was with the police.

As he walked to the door, I could see his eyes moving from corner to corner without moving his head an inch. This was a man who never missed a thing. I was wondering if it might be Bill Kelly. Even in the south, he was well known for being a great police officer.

I answered his brisk knock and opened the door to let him in. Without any thought, I blurted out, "You aren't the well-known Constable Bill Kelly, are you?"

His eyes softened and he smiled. "You've heard of Bill, have you?"

"Yes sir. There were a few stories that made their way to the south."

He laughed. "No, I'm Jim Mclean. Bill is down east now. Just reassigned too."

I must have looked disappointed because he said, "I hope I'll do."

"Oh yes, sir. It was mostly just curiosity on my part anyway. What's the news, Mr. Mclean?"

"Let's sit down, Patrick."

"Yes, sir. Sorry for my bad manners."

I pulled out a kitchen chair for him and then sat down on the one across from him.

"We've completed the autopsy on the remains that were found in the woods here." He pulled out a black and white photo from the large brown envelope he'd been holding. "You mentioned that your grandfather had a foot injury. Would you look at this to see if you think this could be consistent with that accident?"

I looked down at the picture. The bones in the picture were obviously of someone's foot and it was easy to see the damage done by a bullet.

I nodded. "It could easily be. He shattered his foot pretty bad."

"Did he have a limp after the accident?"

"Yes. It didn't slow him down too much but if he was tired, it would bother him."

He put the photo back into the envelope and brought out another one. From it, he pulled out a piece of torn cloth.

"Have you ever seen this cloth before? Could it have been from any of your father's or grandfather's shirts?"

I held the cloth in my hand and looked at it. It was a small dirty and worn piece of blue and white checkered cotton.

I shook my head. "I don't recall my father or grandfather ever wearing checkered shirts. I could almost say with certainty that this wouldn't be from anything they would wear. Did you find this with the bones?"

"No, this doesn't match any of the material that was found with the bodies. We found this caught in a tree branch. We believe it might have been left by someone leaving the area in a hurry."

I stared at him. "You mean this could be from the killer's shirt?"

He nodded. "It could be. And, I'm sorry but you said it correctly when you said 'killer.' The coroner's report states that both men were shot. There's evidence that they were murdered."

He stopped for a few seconds; I imagine waiting to see my reaction. I was sure there had been foul play but it was the first time someone had said outright - someone had murdered my father and grandfather. I could have asked how they knew it was murder but I didn't want to know the details. Not yet.

"I'm very sorry to bring you this news."

"I know. I was expecting it but it still comes as a shock. I can't understand why anyone would want to take their lives. They were such nonviolent men. Even our neighbors used to call them the 'gentlemen' farmers." I shook my head. "None of it makes sense."

"I know, but think, Patrick, could you tell me anything about your father's life? I know this is hard for you but is there anyone who might want him dead and if so, why? Was there a fight over land? Over cattle? Anything?"

I stared at him. "I can't think of anyone who would want to kill my father. He was a hard worker and spent all his time on this farm, working day and night. I can't see any reason why anyone would want him dead."

"Your neighbor says that a man came by looking for him. Do you have any idea who that could be?"

I shook my head. "I've been trying to figure that out too. It sounds like a stranger to me so what would he want with my father and grandfather? I have no idea what all this means."

"I know you've been away for awhile now. Your father never contacted you? Perhaps there might be something in a letter that would be a clue."

"I wish that were so. Apparently, my father did write to me but the man I was working for never gave the letters to me. The letters all came back and they're in my father's desk."

He didn't say anything; just looked at me with a questioning look in his eyes.

"It's a long story, sir, but the man I worked for, my father-in-law, had no use for me."

He nodded as if to say he understood. "We'll have to check all of those letters and anything else that we hope might give us some answers. Later today, someone will be coming in to go through everything in the house."

"I understand, sir. Will I be able to have my father's letters back?"

"Of course, Patrick. If you want to stay you can or it might be easier for you to wait outside." He smiled. "It can be upsetting to watch a search."

"Yes, I think I'll take Toby away from here."

"That might be a good idea. And, Patrick, you said the letters that your father wrote to you were all returned to your father, unread. How could something like this happen? You mean you never saw these letters until now?"

I could feel the tears forming but I could also see Toby watching me so I fought them back.

I shook my head. "No, sir, I never received any of the letters that my father wrote to me except for one. You see, Molly Jordan and I fell in love. She was Jacob Jordan's only child and I guess he thought she could do better. Besides that, we were very young. When we ran away and got married, he wasn't too happy about it. I'm sure that's why he wanted to hurt me. He could do this by blocking me off from my father." I shrugged, "That's the only reason I can think of."

"And where is your wife now?"

I cleared my throat. "She died, sir. She died after giving birth to our son. Our son was born dead. They called it stillborn. Mr. Jordan blamed me for his daughter's death and for his grandchild's death. He even burned the little cabin down that we lived in. He came after me with his shotgun and I had to escape for my life. I went to work for another farmer - a Mr. Pike. He's the one who thought I should take the summer off and come up here to see my father and find out why I hadn't heard from him. I believe he thought it would help me to get away for awhile too."

The officer was silent for a moment. "You say you escaped for your life. Did he threaten you?"

I nodded. "Oh yes, sir. He had an old shotgun and threatened a few times. Either his wife or a neighbor would always step in and talk some sense into him. Otherwise, I probably wouldn't be here today. And, if truth were told, at the time I really didn't care if he had killed me. I was suffering the same as he was."

"I'm sorry for your loss, Patrick. When was it that your wife and child died?"

This time, I couldn't stop the tears. They rolled down my face as I spoke. "It hasn't even been a year yet , sir." I reached up and wiped the tears with my shirtsleeve. "It seems like some nightmare that I had yesterday though."

"Do you think your father-in-law could have known that you were coming up to see your father?"

I shrugged. "Probably. Southern Saskatchewan goes on forever but most folks know what their neighbors are all doing. I'm sure Mrs. Pike, the wife of the man I was working for now, would've told Molly's mother."

He looked down at his notepad and wrote a few more items.

"Could you give me those letters that your father wrote to you that were returned?"

"Yes, sir. They're here in the desk." I walked into the living room and he followed. Toby walked to the door opening and watched.

I took the letters, bound by an elastic band, and handed them to the officer.

"And I imagine you must have written to your father. Have you found any of those?"

I shook my head. "Yes, I did write. I couldn't understand why he didn't answer especially when I told him that I was going to marry Molly. I thought maybe he was disappointed in me. We were so young and it was the first time I was away from home. You know, maybe he was feeling a little like Molly's father was. But then when I wrote about the baby coming and then another letter when Molly died, I still never heard from him. That bothered me."

"So where are the letters that you wrote your father? I'm sure if he kept all of these, he would have kept all yours too."

I shook my head. "I didn't find them anywhere. I would think they would be with these ones but they weren't."

"What do you think could have happened to them?"

"I thought about that and wondered what could have happened but then I remembered that I had never mailed any of my letters. Molly's father always made sure to go into town to pick up the mail and mail any letters that we had. In fact, the one kind thing he did for me was tell me that he would pay for the postage and not to worry."

He nodded. "Thank you, Patrick." He held out his hand and we shook hands. "We'll do all we can to find out who is responsible for your father and grandfather's death."

Before he went out the door, he stopped and asked, "By the way, when your wife died, where did you go immediately afterwards?"

I could feel warmth slowly moving up my face and knew my skin was turning red. It was something that was an embarrassment to me but, as time went by, I realized that there was no reason to feel that way. I was a boy who had gone through a terrible ordeal. Not only had I lost someone

I cared for so deeply, I feared for my own life. My mind kept racing back and forth from wanting to escape death to wanting to welcome it and get it all over.

"Well, sir, I sort of disappeared for a couple of months. I knew of an old abandoned homestead about a day's ride away and I hid out there. The folks who'd lived there couldn't make a go of it anymore so when they pulled out, they left behind what they couldn't take. The old potbellied stove was there and a few dishes and pans so I survived. Afterwards, my mind was better so that's when I found the job with Mr. Pike."

"No one knew where you were?"

I shook my head. "I don't think so. There wasn't a town nearby for miles and even the road going past the house wasn't used anymore." I paused and looked at him. "But sir, if you're thinking that Jacob Jordan came up here to find me, I don't think he would've shot my folks. He hated me but I don't think that he was a killer. Besides, if it was the man who stopped at the Yake's place, that didn't sound like Mr. Jordan at all."

"I appreciate your thoughts, Patrick." He smiled. "Don't worry; we have to check into everything."

When Toby and I went outside, we could see three cars pulled over in the ditch watching the house so we decided to head out to the backfield instead. I'd noticed a patch of blueberry bushes north of the house about a mile away, so we grabbed a couple of pails from the barn and set out across the meadow. Even with all the dry weather, it was a good year for the berries. We ate our share plus more and filled both pails. I would cook them up with some sugar and that would keep us going for a few days. I was only wishing I knew how to make pies.

Three hours later, we made our way back to the house. It was a relief to see that everyone had left - the police and the gawkers. As I looked around at the quiet surroundings, it seemed this was surely only a dream. Toby and I would settle in to our meal, and then I'd hear Pa and Grandpa tramping up to the door, knocking off the dust and manure from their boots, and yelling if supper was ready.

Sadly, that was not the reality. There were too many unanswered questions. I had to find out who murdered my father and grandfather and why. Why would someone kill two unarmed decent human beings? Two men who had never harmed anyone in their lives. What had the killer or killers wanted from them?

I would take Toby back to his grandmother and then make it my pursuit to find a murderer. I would hunt down that person, as Jacob Jordan had hunted me down. I was never a vengeful person but when I told myself that, I felt as if I had a purpose in life.

Chapter Twenty Nine

With so many concerns on my mind, I'd forgotten about the farm. What was to become of it? Did it belong to me now? How many years had my father not paid his taxes? Had he finally listened to my mother's wisdom and opened a bank account?

Before I could go anywhere, I knew I would have to get all this settled. It wasn't like Winnipesaukee who had been a squatter and owned nothing. This might be more complicated. Perhaps, there was some merit in squatting and owning nothing.

The next morning, as I was having my first cup of coffee in the kitchen, Toby wandered in from his bedroom, rubbing sleep from his eyes.

"Are we leaving today, Patrick? Do you think we could stay a few days longer? My grandma could probably use the rest, you know."

I smiled at the boy with his long black tousled hair and bright blue eyes. He was wearing one of my grandfather's gray flannel shirts and the shirttail almost dragged on the floor as he walked. Since we'd both finally had our baths before bed, we were both looking, smelling, and feeling much better.

I shook my head. "Not today, Toby. We'll have to ride over to Mr. Yake's place sometime this morning. I have some questions for him. It might be a while before we can leave because I'll have to figure out what to do with this farm."

His eyes lit up. "Maybe we could live here? I would love to live here on the farm with you, Patrick. Could we, please?"

"No, Toby, we won't be living here. We could never make a living on this land. Besides, I don't think I'd make a good farmer. You belong with your grandma and I have to get back to Mr. Pike's as soon as I can."

"I thought you were going to be a teacher. Why couldn't we live here and you could teach in a school." His eyes lit up. "This could be the school."

I laughed. "I'm a long way from being a school teacher, Toby. A person has to go to school to learn to teach school. I might never be able to do that."

He blinked away the tears and walked back into the bedroom. In a few minutes, he was back, dressed in his

196

clean pants and shirt. I'd washed our dirty clothes as best as I could and hung them out on the clothes line. Dark clouds were threatening rain but even if it did rain, the clothes could use an extra rinse so I was leaving them where they were.

"Want me to make some hot cakes for breakfast, Toby?"

He grinned and nodded. I was learning that the best way to cheer the boy up was to offer food.

After gobbling up three large hotcakes and swallowing them down with a glass of Carnation evaporated milk mixed with water, Toby was smiling again.

"When are we leaving to see Mr. Yake? Should I go and get Rosie out of the barn?"

"We'll wash up these dishes first, Toby, and then we'll leave."

I was also learning the quickest way to remove a smile from his face was to ask him to help wash dishes.

Before heading over to the train siding, I thought I should see if there were papers that I could show Mr. Yake. Somewhere, there would be a deed to the land or at least something to show my father's ownership. Once again, I went through the papers in the desk drawers. The officers who searched didn't believe in putting everything back in its place so once again, I had to start all over.

Toby sat on the sofa, banging his legs against the frame, anxiously waiting for me to finish.

"Patrick," he said. "Can I go up into the attic to see where you used to sleep?"

My first reaction was to say no but on second thought, I wanted to get on with my job, and the constant banging was getting on my nerves.

"Sure. I'll get the ladder for you."

The batteries in my father's flashlight were dead but there was some light shining up through the opening. Most nights I never had a flashlight and I seemed to manage as a kid.

I went back to checking through my father's papers and could hear Toby bumping and thumping above me. If he were lucky, he might come across an old toy that I had as a young boy. Or some hidden school work that I never completed.

It was about ten minutes later that I hear loud scrambling above me. It sounded like Toby was crawling from one end of the attic to the other at a very fast speed. My first thoughts were of mice, as I knew that as the summer wound down, the little critters liked to find a warm home for the winter too.

I thought he was going to fall through the opening so I jumped up to grab him if need be. But Toby didn't fall through the hole in the ceiling; as I gazed up, I saw the brown paper bag that Toby was holding rip open and money in the form of paper bills floated down around me.

Chapter Thirty

"Where did my father's cattle go?" I asked Henry Yake.

Toby and I had a talk before we left and I told him in a very serious tone, we were not to discuss the money that he'd found in the attic. I had to sort things out, one mystery at a time.

Henry stopped and stared at me. We were standing in the small room that was used for obtaining train tickets, buying or trading food stuffs, or sitting on the three chairs along the wall to get out of the rain or snow while either waiting for the train or waiting for someone to pick you up. Since the roads in winter and spring were impassable, many people in the area used the train to get to the nearest town. When I was a small boy, I loved coming here. As I grew older, the room grew smaller and smaller. Now it looked cramped and messy. While Henry's wife was alive, she made sure it looked inviting.

"I don't know. I always thought he'd gone to stay with you so someone must be looking after the cattle. You didn't see any wandering around?" He stopped talking and put his hand on his chin. "You look over the fence to see what Becker's got over on his side?"

I shook my head. "I'm sure Mr. Becker didn't steal our cattle. Could someone else?"

"North of you, there's nothing but bush and the government's been trying to get rid of that land for years. You think your pa and grandpa could've taken them to market?"

I shrugged. "I don't know. I could check though. Do you know whom I should contact?"

He nodded. "I'm going into town tomorrow. Why don't you let me check it out for you? I'll stop by your place on my way home."

"Thanks, Mr. Yake. I appreciate it."

"No problem. Why don't you and the young fellow come inside and have a cup of coffee with me? I think I can maybe even find some cocoa." He looked at Toby. "How would you like some cocoa?"

Toby just grinned.

It was mid-afternoon by the time we arrived back at the house. There was still smoke trickling out the chimney from the morning's fire and it seemed more like my old home. I almost forgot for a moment that it wasn't the same and would never be again. I tried not to appear too worried when I was with Toby. My murdered parent and grandparent did fill my mind though. Sometimes, I reasoned that perhaps Jacob Jordan hired a killer to come and kill my folks, reasoning that he wanted me to hurt, as he was hurting. Surely, he couldn't be that wicked though.

Now there was all that money to wonder about. Where had it come from? The first thing I was going to do when we got in the door was go up into the attic to see if Toby had missed something. I had taken the time to count it and there was close to one hundred dollars. Never in my life had I seen so much money at one time. After counting it, I took it into the kitchen and hid it in a tin can with a tight lid on it. Before leaving, I placed it into the bucket at the well and lowered it down on a rope. The water level was still low from the drought so the tin hung just above the water line. When Toby brought up water, he used a smaller bucket with a longer rope, and it dropped below the water's surface. He was a strong little kid and had no problem turning the handle and hoisting up the bucket.

After putting the buggy back into the barn, I left Toby to look after Rosie and I went into the house. This time I remembered to get a battery from Henry Yake so I could take a flashlight up into the attic. As I climbed up, I thought about all those years that I climbed the same ladder. The attic, where it was freezing cold in winter - frost covered the wooden boards above me and no matter how many featherbeds my mother heaped on top of me, I still shivered, and so hot in summer that sweat rolled off my body and I thought my blood would boil.

I pulled myself up into a sitting position and shone the flashlight around the room. The highest peak was about six feet high but the rest of the ceiling was low so there was no room for walking around. I started out crawling and shining the light on every inch as I went. There was a layer of straw on top of the wood for insulation so as I went I moved it to see if there was anything underneath. In the farthest northeast corner, I could see where Toby had moved the straw and found the bag of money. I stayed there, carefully moving the straw in every direction to see if there was anything under it. Or, perhaps, something had fallen out of the bag.

I could see nothing and had almost given up when I spotted a small piece of paper pushed up against a board. Perhaps it was nothing. There was writing on it but in pencil and the light wasn't strong enough for me to read all of it. One thing that stood out was my name. My first thought was that it might be some old paper from my school days and a feeling of disappointment went through me. Please, I prayed to no one in particular because I wasn't sure about God anymore, help me solve this mystery. Please, let me find out who killed my father and grandfather.

I scrambled down the ladder and went over to the desk. Toby wasn't back in the house so I checked out the window and saw that he was busy brushing Rosie down. That horse had never been brushed so much in her life and she was relishing every minute.

I sat in the chair and unfolded the paper. I did it very slowly because I was sure it would be nothing and that I would end up disappointed again. My name was on the outside and inside, my father had written a note for me. My heart pounded as I read it.

Dear son, it said, *Grandpa and I are worried about you. We haven't heard anything and my letters have been returned. I sold all the cattle and some of the farm equipment and have paid up the taxes for the farm so we don't have to worry about them and we are coming south to look for you. The fellow who bought the cattle is coming out today to get them so we will leave tomorrow. If you happen to get home while we're away, I am going to leave this on the table for you. We hope nothing terrible has happened. While I'm writing this, I might as well tell you that if anything happens to me or your grandpa, the farm is yours. Your father, James Edward Smithson.*

I'm sure my heart stopped beating. This answered some of the questions. The money came from selling off the cattle and what little equipment my dad owned. It also touched my heart. My father cared enough for me that he would sell everything so he could go out and hunt for me. Tears rolled down my cheek. How did I never realize what love he had for me? Now, I had lost Molly and my parents. Would I ever find anyone who could love me this much again?

Chapter Thirty One

The next morning, the RCMP were back at the house. Toby watched in wonderment as the two men walked to the door. I couldn't help be impressed by the red uniform and polished boots myself. I opened the door before they knocked.

"Are you any closer to solving my father's and grandfather's murder?" I asked.

"Let's sit down, Mr. Smithson," the older man said. "Why don't we sit at the kitchen table?"

After settling in, the same gentleman said, "We've been questioning the man you used to work for - a Mr. Jacob Jordan."

"You went all the way down there to question him?" I was stunned.

He nodded. "We have a double murder to solve, Patrick. This isn't something the RCMP take lightly. We'll go to the ends of the earth if need be to find a killer. Why are you so surprised?"

I shrugged. "I don't know. It's hard to imagine that Mr. Jordan would come all the way here to kill my family. Except me, of course. I could see him killing me. Unless he came to kill me and maybe got into a fight with my father? Something like that?"

The officer shook his head. "No, Jacob Jordan isn't a suspect any longer. He hasn't left southern Saskatchewan. In fact, I don't know if you know this or not but he is not a well man."

"He's sick? I didn't know that."

"His wife says that since their daughter and grandson died, her husband has given up on life. He hasn't looked after his farm and that, combined with the drought, has left them penniless."

"I'm sorry. I didn't realize that. You said he was sick though."

The officer lifted his hand and pointed to his head. "Up here. He has been in an institution for the past few months. We talked to the doctor and he said that Mr. Jordan had tried to commit suicide at least three times. Each time, the doctors gave him some pills for depression and sent him home. Now, he's in an asylum in Regina and will probably never get out."

I knew I should have some sympathy for the man, but when it came to Jacob Jordan, my heart was stone.

"And Mrs. Jordan?"

"She has gone to Swift Current and is living with relatives."

"I'm sorry to hear that. I never meant to hurt those people. I just fell in love with their daughter. That's all."

"Patrick, Mrs. Jordan understands that. She asked about you and feels sorry for how she and her husband treated you. Mr. Jordan is now suffering because of his actions and nothing can bring his mind back. He is getting shock treatments but nothing seems to work. This isn't your fault, Patrick, and don't ever think that it is. You had your own sorrow to deal with and you were able to handle it better. Leave it at that."

Those were kind words and eventually they would reach my heart and I would understand. However, some scars take many years to heal no matter how hard you work at them.

"There's something else I should show you, sir." I reached into my shirt pocket, pulled out my father's note, and handed it to him.

He slowly unfolded it and read it.

"When did you find this?"

"Just now."

"Where was it? My men searched thoroughly but didn't find any note."

"It was up in the attic along with the money. The money is in a tin can in the well if you want to see it."

He reread the note.

"He doesn't say who bought the cattle."

I shook my head. "No. I have no idea who it might be. Do you think they might have some information about the murders?"

"Well, it appears they would be the last ones to see your father and grandfather alive. Did you find anything else up there?"

"No, sir."

"It looks to me that whoever bought the cattle paid for them first and then came to pick them up. Obviously, they took the cattle or the cattle would still be here. If they came and left, your father would have put the note on the table and in the morning, he and your grandfather would have left. Either the ones who came for the cattle killed them or someone came right after they left."

"Do you think they came for the money?"

He nodded slowly. "That would be my guess. I don't see any other reason for coming."

"Do you think my father refused to give them the money so they shot him?"

"It looks that way to me. Perhaps your father became suspicious and hid the money up in the attic when he saw them returning."

My stubborn father and even more stubborn grandfather had given their lives for a bag of money. Once again, I felt a burden thrown upon my shoulders. Why hadn't I come sooner? When Molly and I first married, I should have brought her home to meet my family. The reason I hadn't come was because I was angry that my dad hadn't answered my letters. It was difficult for me to forgive Jacob Jordan and if he had lost his mind, it was less than what he deserved.

Chapter Thirty Two

Henry Yake arrived late in the afternoon. We always knew when a vehicle was coming down the road because we could see dust rising in the air from miles away. Toby, who had been bringing water up for Rosie, stopped and waited to see who was coming into the yard. Ever since the cup of hot cocoa, Henry was Toby's new friend. I waited inside until the dust had cleared.

"So, Mr. Yake," I said. "Were you able to find out anything about the cattle? I think I might have sent you on a wild goose chase. The RCMP believe my father sold them privately and perhaps, the buyer came back to steal the money."

He shook his head. "No, the RCMP knows now what happened. I was at the stockyard when they questioned Bill Mathers. Your father sold the cattle and got a fair price for them. In fact, your father started pretty high but the fellow never argued."

"Who was this fellow?"

He shrugged. "Bill said he never saw him before. He said he had a ranch close to the Manitoba border but I'd say it was probably in the opposite direction."

"Bill didn't go out to the farm to check on the cattle?"

"The next day he was going to send one of his boys out to round up the cattle but the owner said not to bother, that he had enough riders to get it done. Since Bill didn't hear anything more, he figured the cattle had been delivered and the owner was pleased. Your dad told him he was travelling south to visit you so that's why no one has been worried."

"So whoever bought the cattle decided to end up with the cattle and get his money back too. Toby discovered that bag of money up in the attic."

He nodded. "Guess your pa wasn't about to go along with his plan. He must have been a bit suspicious of those men; otherwise, he wouldn't have hidden the money."

"It wasn't worth losing his life over though."

"No, it wasn't."

"Think they'll ever find the killer?"

He grinned. "You know what they say, 'the Mounties always get their man.'"

I returned his smile. "I hope so. I wonder how many other farmers they've done this to and gotten away with it."

He reached over and patted my shoulder. "Don't worry, son. They'll find out who did this." He stopped and looked out over the field, deep in thought. "You know, I think the time is coming when a handshake isn't going to be worth a plug nickel."

"I hope you're wrong, Henry."

Before getting into his car, he called out to Toby, "Hey, Toby, I got something for you."

Toby raced over and Henry Yake handed him a string of licorice. If I'd thought he was pleased with cocoa, that was nothing compared to licorice.

Three days later, the same RCMP officer drove into the yard. For the first time since I'd met him, he looked relaxed and wore a smile. We shook hands and I invited him in.

"Were you planning on leaving, Patrick?" he asked when he saw a pile of supplies sitting on the floor.

"I hope it's okay. I do have to get Toby home and I'm hoping my job is still there, waiting for me."

"No, you're free to leave. I thought you might like to know that we have caught the men who tried to rob your father."

"And killed him?"

He nodded. "Yes, and killed him and your grandfather."

"You said 'men.' Was there more than one?"

"There's a band of them. They scout out the area when they hear that someone is talking about selling their stock and then they set the plan in motion."

"Do you think the man who talked to the Beckers was scouting my father out?"

"That seems to be their pattern. We checked out another case west of here and found out some interesting things. Someone in the Battleford area knew his neighbor was selling off some of his cattle. Times are hard so he needed the money to buy feed for the winter for the remaining stock he had left. However, something didn't seem right with this neighbor. He noticed the man had less stock but he didn't seem to have any feed for the ones he still had. It didn't sit right with him so he went to the detachment and spoke to a constable there. The officer went out to check on the man but he denied everything. Said all was well. That he'd put the money in the bank and that his neighbor was too nosey and that it was none of his business."

"How did you find out then that he'd been robbed?"

"He had no money in the bank. Also, his wife broke down and confessed that they'd been robbed and that the men had threatened their lives. They have a son going to school in Saskatoon and they said if they went to the police, something would happen to their son."

"Did they know the men's names? Is that how you caught them?"

"Oh no, they're too smart to give their real names; however, they were too stupid to not check to see if the cattle were branded. These crooks never kept the cattle; they took them to different stockyards or sold them privately. We were able to find the branded cattle and although they gave a false name, they didn't realize that the buyer wrote down the truck's license number. He said he was a little suspicious about the men."

"Where are they now?"

"Now, they are in custody in a Saskatoon prison, awaiting trial."

"Will I be needed to testify?"

"I don't believe so but we will need the note your father wrote."

"Will you need the money?"

He smiled. "I'm sure you can use that money, can't you, Patrick?"

I nodded. "Well, I don't have any other."

He laughed. "Could you show it to me and then I can testify that it does exist and that your father received payment for those cattle. Even though we have no idea what happened to the cattle in the last year, the money rightfully belongs to you."

It was another one of those moments when I felt a load lifted off my shoulders. Now it felt like my father and grandfather were heroes. They did not give in to those thugs. If it hadn't been for them, these men might have gone on to swindle many more and who knows? Perhaps, they had murdered more than just them.

"Do you think they killed anyone else?" I asked.

"They could have. We're looking into it."

I glanced over at the cook stove.

"Would you like a cup of coffee?"

He grinned. "I thought you'd never ask. I could smell it as I was walking to the door."

We spent some time talking about the work of the Royal Canadian Mounted Police and no mention was made of cattle rustlers or killers. I called Toby in because I knew he would love to listen. After the constable left, he said, "That's what I'm going to be when I grow up."

Toby didn't realize that when he went with his grandmother, they would be traveling back to the United States. There would be no RCMP there but I didn't want to destroy a young boy's dream.

"That's a good goal to have, Toby," was all I said.

"What about you, Patrick? Are you going to work on that farm all your life or are you going to come back here and work on your own farm?"

That was food for thought. I now had some money and owned a farm. But was I cut out to be a farmer? That was the question.

Chapter Thirty Three

Toby and I set out three days later for Qu'Appelle Valley. It was only the third week in August but again there hadn't been enough rain and the Poplar leaves were turning yellow. In many ways, I was feeling sad about leaving but I knew I couldn't stay and I couldn't come back to live. Henry Yake was going to try to sell the farm for me. I gave him Mr. Pike's address if he needed to communicate with me. I was quite sure Mr. Pike wouldn't be getting a telephone anytime soon. Henry gave me his telephone number if I needed to talk to him in an emergency. I'd never talked on a telephone but I was sure that someday every business owner would probably have one.

Instead of sharing Rosie's back this time, we left in the buggy. We had room for plenty of supplies and if it rained during the night, we could sleep under the buggy. I bought a rubber sheet from Henry so we had that in case it rained during the day. There was no rush so Rosie took her time. When we reached the highway, she sped up but I think it was mostly because she didn't like the cars getting ahead of her. Some of the time, if the ditches were wide, we would take the buggy down into it. When we thought it was noon, we pulled up under a tree and had our lunch. After we ate, we had a quick nap before starting up again. Toby wasn't in total agreement with the nap part but he usually fell asleep before I did.

As the scenery changed and the trees started getting sparse, Toby became quieter. He knew it would soon be time to see his grandmother, go back to his home, and start school.

"You'll be happy to go back to school, Toby." I tried to encourage him.

"No, I hate school and I'm not good at anything."

"What aren't you good at?"

He thought for a few minutes. "I hate spelling."

I laughed. "Well, that's easily fixed. Memorize how the hard words are spelled and sound out the easy ones."

He shook his head. "I still hate it."

"How will you write up your reports when you're a policeman then?"

He looked at me in horror.

"Policemen have to write reports?"

I nodded. "Of course, didn't you see when they were at the farm that they were always taking notes? How would

216

you feel if you handed your report back to the Commissioner and he couldn't understand what you wrote because your spelling was so bad?"

He thought on that for a while. "Maybe I'll be a farmer instead."

"Really? You aren't very committed, are you?"

"What do you mean?"

"Well, if you are determined to do or be something, then you should stick to your decision. You won't get anywhere in the world if you keep hopping from one decision to another."

"Maybe I don't want to get anywhere in this world. Maybe I just want to be happy."

"It's okay to be happy, Toby, but you have to have some purpose in your life. You don't have to be rich but you should find something to do that makes you happy but also helps others."

"Is that what you are going to do, Patrick?"

"That is what I have to start doing. I've been wasting my time." I smiled at him. "I think I have to start taking my own advice."

He grinned. "Are you going to be a teacher?"

I laughed. "That's what Winnipesaukee thought I should be. For some reason, he thought I'd be good teaching young boys." I looked over at him. "What do you think?"

He smiled. "I think you're good with me and I'm a boy."

"Well, that's all I needed to hear. I will be a teacher and teach boys how to spell."

Toby laughed so hard I thought he was going to fall out of the buggy.

Chapter Thirty Four

When we approached the bridge over the Qu'Appelle River, I pulled Rosie off into the ditch on the left and even though there was no trail for a buggy but only a walking path, we followed it. There must have been a downpour the day before because the ground was soggy and the wheels made ruts as we went. The river lapped against the shore and again we could hear the lonesome call of the loon. It was late afternoon and the trees cast shadows on the water. Soon we came to Winnipesaukee's cabin. It sat there as we had left it. I pulled Rosie closer. The same ashes from the last log I'd burned still filled the fire pit.

"Do you want to come in?" I asked Toby.

He shook his head. "Can I go in by myself?"

I nodded. "I understand. I want to check to make sure no one has ransacked the place. Then you can go in."

I pushed the door open. The air smelled stale as it does when all the doors and windows are shut for several days. Everything was the same as I'd left it. The thought did come to me that the only option left was to burn it to the ground. No one would ever live here again. I wouldn't want anyone to. It would be intruding on Sarah and Frank's life. It seemed strange thinking of Winnipesaukee as Frank Lawdry but that's who he was - Frank Lawdry, great great grandfather to Tobias Lawdry, the little boy sitting out in the wagon. If only Tobias could hear Frank Lawdry's life story. Was I the only one who had heard it? Yes, I was and I knew already I'd forgotten most of it. Sadness and despair had filled and overtaken my mind. If only I still had all the stories that I wrote night after night for Molly during our first winter together - our first and only winter.

After one last glance around the cabin, I pulled the door shut and climbed back into the buggy.

"You want to go in now, Toby?"

He nodded. While I waited, I looked out over the river. It was so easy to see why Sarah had picked this spot to build her home. I wondered if it had brought her true happiness.

In a few minutes, Toby joined me and we made our way to his place. His grandmother heard us coming and she was standing on the porch, waiting. I hardly recognized her. She'd put on weight and there was color in her cheeks.

Her eyes lit up when she saw her grandson. "Toby, you are back home." She ran to meet us with her arms outspread. "Oh Toby, I've missed you so much."

220

Before the buggy had come to a complete stop, Toby was out of it and in his grandmother's arms. Tears were running down her face as she kissed his cheeks, over and over again.

I guess she realized she might be embarrassing the boy by all the affection so she quickly stood up and wiped her eyes. Toby, it seemed didn't mind at all as he clung to his grandmother.

"Oh goodness, Mr. Smithson, please step down. You have no idea how happy I am to see the two of you. I have been so worried. The RCMP came around asking questions and even though they said there was nothing to worry about, you know it's hard not to."

"The RCMP were here?"

She nodded, all the time stroking Toby's head. "They were wondering something about your father's farm. I had no idea what they were talking about. However, they did tell me about your father and grandfather, Patrick, and I'm so sorry. You've had much heartache in your life - as it seems so many of us have. Anyway, they just wanted to make sure Toby was my grandson and assured me that he was all right. So, as you can imagine, I've been waiting every day and watching to see you coming down this path."

As soon as Toby heard RCMP, he perked up. "Grandma, that's what I want to be when I grow up."

"What, dearie?"

"An RCMP."

She looked up at me and smiled. "Well, you could do much worse, Toby. Now, come inside and have something to eat."

We sat in comfort in the small kitchen. Toby and I were hungry, tired, and covered in dust from the long ride. Toby made sure that Rosie was watered and fed. It was already dark by the time we'd finished eating.

"Patrick, I fixed up a bed for you in the shed. I hope you'll be comfortable there. You are welcome to stay as long as you like. I think Toby and I will stay for the winter and then leave for Montana in the spring."

"Montana. That brings back memories from Winnipesaukee's story. I remember that his sister, Sarah, lived by the Milk River for quite a few years in a Métis settlement before she discovered the Qu'Appelle valley. She was searching for a valley with a river running through." I looked out the window into the moonlit night. "It seems sort of surreal that this was the spot she was dreaming about."

"What does that mean, Patrick?" Toby piped up.

"What does what mean?"

"That word - surreal."

"It can mean strange or dreamlike." I reached over and ruffled his hair. "But I'm not going to spell it for you. You can find a dictionary and learn yourself."

"I don't have a dictionary."

"Well, you do now. I bought one for Winnipesaukee but now it will belong to you."

Lilly laughed. "You're going to make a scholar out of him yet, Patrick." She started clearing the dishes off the table and putting them in the dishpan on the stove. "I'm sure you are both tired. Perhaps you should stay a few days and rest up before your long drive."

"I reckon I could sleep standing up, Miss Lilly. I appreciate your kindness. I've sent a letter to Mr. Pike, however, saying I was on my way home so I best be leaving in the morning. It's still a long drive with the horse and buggy."

She smiled. "I understand. You have no idea how much I appreciate you taking Toby with you this summer. It was good for both of you, I think."

I nodded. I didn't say anything but she was right. Toby kept me going. If it weren't for that little boy, I would have been somewhere at the bottom of a lake and no one would have known.

Toby and I never showed much affection toward each other but that night, I hugged him and said goodbye.

"Thank Patrick for taking you with him, Toby," his grandmother said.

Toby looked up at me with tears in his eyes and quivering lips but no sound came out. He raced out the door and into the darkness.

"Oh that boy! He'll be the death of me yet," Lilly said, but there was a smile on her lips.

I found my way to the shed in the moonlight. I heard Rosie nickering and I knew where Toby was. He would probably spend the night with Rosie.

As soon as the sky in the east turned slightly red, I was up and ready to leave. Lilly came out and brought a sack of food for me. I appreciated it and thanked her. Never would I mention that I had enough money packed in my suitcase to eat in restaurants all along the way. Even fancy ones if I so chose.

When I entered the shed-like barn where Rosie had spent the night, I saw Toby fast asleep in the straw. Rosie whinnied when she saw me, and Toby opened his eyes.

Toby jumped up and ran out the door. I knew that would be the last time I would see him.

I took my time hitching Rosie up to the buggy so Toby could get his last look at us from the hedge where I was sure he was hiding.

On the way to the main road, I stopped once again for the last time in front of Winnipesaukee's cabin. This time I got out of the buggy and went inside. I gathered as much paper as I could find, piled it under the old wooden table, and threw a match into it. The ground was still muddy so I wasn't worried about all of Saskatchewan going up in flames.

By the time, I reached the road and crossed the bridge I could see smoke billowing into the sky. In my mind's eye, I could see the grin on Toby's face.

Chapter Thirty Five

Mr. and Mrs. Pike were pleased to see me but I knew there wasn't much work for me and even if there were, they had no money to pay me. What was I to do with my life? I couldn't live on my father's money forever - even though a hundred dollars during the Great Depression was a windfall.

"Why don't you stay for the winter, Patrick?" Mr. Pike sat in this big chair, tapping this pipe on his teeth. "You got nowhere to go and here you can at least have food to eat and a roof over your head."

I hadn't told anyone about the money. Even Toby would have no idea how much and if he had overheard me speak of it with Henry Yake, he wouldn't realize the value. Seventy-five years later that $100.00 would be worth about $2000.00. Back then, ham was 39 cents a pound; a dozen eggs cost 18 cents, and bananas were 19 cents for four pounds but most folks couldn't even afford that.

."You've been so kind to me, Mr. Pike. If I stay the winter, I can at least cut down brush for you so you can have enough wood for the stove. I'll feed the livestock every day for you too. I'll earn my keep."

He nodded. "Aye, that would be a big help. Farming's starting to get a bit too much for me. And, seeing what's happened to your pa and grandpa, I don't think it's good for you to be alone for the time being. Sometimes it takes a while for a shock to set in. You've had your share the past couple of years now."

"Yes, sir. I reckon I have."

"You have to start thinking about your future though. You don't want to be someone who just roams around and ends up without a home. You understand what I'm saying?"

I nodded. "I do understand. I believe I'm going to become a school teacher, Mr. Pike."

Well, the look on that man's face still brings a smile to my lips. Telling a farmer you wanted to be a school teacher was like telling a millionaire you wanted to be a pauper.

After letting it sink in, he said, "I do believe I remember you speaking of it but I thought the fantasy had left your mind. I ain't saying that school teaching is a bad thing. We need teachers; it's just that most teachers are women. You realize that, don't you?"

"Yes, sir, I do but I believe that's mostly with small children. I think I'd like to teach older boys."

"Really? How do you plan on going about doing that? I didn't think you had much schooling."

I shook my head. "I've just got my grade eight but I heard that you can take courses by correspondence."

His eyebrows went up. "Correspondence?"

"By mail. There's a woman in Regina who set that up a few years back. You can take your grades all the way up to grade eleven."

He grunted. "Grade eleven? That's a high grade, son. Most folks don't even need that much education. It can be quite a waste of time, you know. You think you can learn all that through the mail?"

"I'm going to try. Even with grade eleven, I should be able to teach somewhere. Don't you think?"

"Personally, I don't see any need for anyone to get more education than that."

The next day I went into town, taking Mr. Pike's wagon and team of horses. I picked up enough supplies to last for a month and paid for them with my money. Before getting supplies, however, I stopped in at the Post Office to see if anyone there knew about taking correspondence courses.

John Bell and his wife, Elizabeth, knew about it and were excited to share the information. It seemed that I would not be the only one doing it. A young woman who lived farther south and whose parents farmed in 'no man's land' was taking her schooling that way, too. In fact, it seemed most who were taking it were of the female gender. However, I was not deterred. I had to be true to my word to Toby.

"Here you go, Patrick," Mrs. Bell said, as she handed me some papers to fill out and mail in. "This goes right to one of the legislative buildings in Regina. Once they find out how much education you have and how old you are, they'll send out your course for you." She reached over and touched my arm. "We were so sorry to hear about your family and I think it's wonderful that you're going to work hard to improve your way of life."

"You heard about my father and grandfather?"

"Oh yes, the RCMP were here making inquiries." She lowered her voice. "I believe they may have suspected Molly's father. Did they ever find out who did this?"

"Yes, Mrs. Bell, and it had nothing to do with Mr. Jordan. A group of unscrupulous men were stealing money and cattle from farmers. My father refused to give them the money so he and grandpa paid the price." I decided I might as well be open about it because I knew Mrs. Bell was a notorious gossip. "If they hadn't though, the stealing would've kept going on. I miss them but I know they were heroes."

Her eyes watered and she shook her head. "And now we have a war going on and more men are being killed. What's this world coming to anyway?"

She reached over and patted my arm. "I'm so glad that you decided to stay home and not join the army."

As I walked away, I wasn't sure if that should make me feel good or that I'd made the wrong decision.

The Pikes never questioned where the money came from so all winter when I went into town to return my correspondence papers and pick up the new ones, I would also buy supplies. One day, I saw a bolt of cotton on sale and bought a piece big enough for Mrs. Pike to make a dress and have some left over.

"Oh my, Patrick, you shouldn't be spending your money on me." She lifted the material to her cheek. "But it is so soft and lovely." Tears formed. "I don't think I've ever seen such fine cotton before."

Before I could move, she'd turned and planted a kiss on my cheek and without a word, she rushed into the bedroom with her new material and shut the door.

"Ah, now, you've softened that old woman's heart," Mr. Pike said, grinning with his pipe sticking out the side of his mouth.

"She deserves it," I said. "She's been like a mother to me."

I do believe Mrs. Pike heard that from her bedroom because from that day on, as the saying goes, she spoiled me rotten.

I worked hard on my schoolwork. Winter came and, as usual, it was cold with blowing snow and icy roads. Every afternoon after the chores were finished and long into the night, by the light from a coal oil lamp, I worked on my correspondence course. Mrs. Pike made sure I had plenty of coffee and cocoa to drink and often yelled at Mr. Pike to stoke the fire so I wouldn't get a chill. By spring, I had successfully completed my grade eleven.

But how was I going to teach school? If I went into Moose Jaw to attend Normal School, I would need to have my grade twelve. After spending so much time and learning more than I had in the eight years I attended school, I was tired of being a student. I wanted to be a teacher.

One day in late spring when thoughts were turning to spring seeding, I saw a notice in the local store. A small one-room school situated south of Swift Current, not far from the American border, needed a teacher. The notice said there was a small room at the back of the school that served as the teacher's residence and a barn for the students' and the teacher's horses. The wages were pathetic but it was just what I wanted. I also knew they would be desperate for a teacher. No one in his right mind would want to live in the middle of nowhere all alone. I quickly sent off a reply, along with my qualifications, and three weeks later, I received my answer.

I was now a schoolteacher.

Chapter Thirty Six

You would have thought Mr. and Mrs. Pike were my parents the way they bragged about me to everyone they met. Mrs. Pike, who once could hardly stand being in the same room as me, now clucked over me like a mother hen.

"You'll need some new clothes for your job, Patrick. We'll have to watch for sales in the Eaton's Catalogue. Even if you have only one set, you can always wash them up on the weekend. Mr. Pike has some shirts that don't fit him anymore and I can fix those up for you."

I smiled at her. "Don't be fussing, Mrs. Pike. I won't be leaving until the end of August so there's lots of time."

She nodded. "Oh, I know but I don't want to be rushing. I'll work on them during the summer."

Then one day, there was a letter for me at the Post Office. It was from Henry Yake. Someone wanted to buy the farm. I signed all the papers and sent them back before returning home. I must have been beaming when I walked in the door because both Mr. and Mrs. Pike stood staring at me with expectant looks on their faces.

I held up the personal letter Henry had sent. "Someone is buying my father's farm!"

We celebrated that night with a bottle of chokecherry wine that Mrs. Pike had hidden away in the back of the cupboard.

"I was saving this for just such an occasion," she said.

It was the end of July and I'd almost given up on receiving anything from the farm when the check arrived. I couldn't hide it under the mattress with the other money. Now for the first time in my life, I knew I would have to open a bank account. Not that I received a huge settlement from the sale of the farm - my father paid twenty-five dollars an acre and because of the ten year drought and the war, I received even less, but it was off my hands now. After paying a lawyer, some back taxes, and giving Henry something for all his time and work, I didn't get rich from it. At least, my father and grandfather had cleared most of the bush so the new owners could begin planting their crops in the spring.

It was now 1940, and the war was in full swing so most of the government's money was going for that. I still had mixed feelings about it. My parents often spoke about what happened in London during the war and that World War One was the war to end all wars. Never again would the whole world be embroiled in a war that would kill off millions of healthy young men, not to mention innocent women and children. I couldn't understand how there could be so much hatred and prejudice everywhere - even where I lived.

It seemed as if we should have been sheltered from it all. How could the hearts of folks living in a small section of southern Saskatchewan fill with such anger towards a certain race? Neighbors who had once been friends suddenly hated and mistrusted each other. With a knot in my stomach, I watched as a German family drove through town with all their belongings piled high in the back of their truck while bystanders shouted obscenities at them from the sidewalk. Later, I learned that before settling down in another province, they changed their name from Schmidt to Smith.

Thankfully, this was not a regular occurrence and generally, most people kept their opinions to themselves.

Before leaving for my new teaching position, I made my first major purchase. A 1932 used Ford Tudor sedan V8 with a 65 HP engine. The man was selling it because he had enlisted and thought it would be foolish to have it sitting when his young wife could use the money. After taking a few lessons on driving from the owner, I felt as if the car and I were one.

Mr. and Mrs. Pike were as enthralled with my car as I was. Mrs. Pike brought out her camera, which she used only on special occasions as the film was getting more and more expensive, and took a picture of me standing beside the car.

Mr. Pike suggested that I deposit my money in a bank in Swift Current so we made a day trip there. I decided to put the money from the sale of the farm in the bank, but pocket the money from the sale of the cattle. I never knew what expenses I might incur and I wasn't entirely comfortable with putting all of it in the bank.

I was happy to make the trip as it was good to take my new car for a long drive. Also, I wanted pick up supplies where I would have a better selection. Mrs. Pike sat in the back seat with her head held high wearing her Sunday best, including a hat with netting over it that she had to dust off before putting on her head. I don't think a smile left her lips for the whole day and when we finally got home after dark, she gave me a hug and a kiss on the cheek before I trudged off to bed.

It was a sad goodbye as I left three days later. Mr. Pike and I spent the last couple of days harvesting the last bit of wheat that was still standing in one field. It was better than the past years and the heads of grain were quite full. I think it was the first time since I'd met him that Mr. Pike had anything positive to say about farming. The years of drought had taken some of the stuffing out of the most devout farmers.

The day I left, my car started without any problems. In fact, it purred as if it were ready to move on too. I gave the Pikes a last wave and drove away. Through my mirror, I could see the outline of Mrs. Pike waving a white tea towel above her head and by the time I reached the main road she was only a speck in the distance. In the back seat, tucked away in an old suitcase were a new suit, three shirts, a cardigan sweater, and long underwear - all from the Eaton's catalogue. Mr. Pike was able to keep all his shirts.

The morning I left, the sun was red in the east and the air was brisk and invigorating. The nights were starting to get cooler and some low-lying areas had received a touch of frost. It was early for frost but we might not get it again until the beginning of November. No one could guess the weather patterns in this part of the country. I wasn't even worrying about the weather that day. Everything, for the first time in a long time, looked rosy. I felt guilty for being so happy and pleased with myself. Sometimes if I spent a whole day not thinking about Molly or my family, I would feel terrible. How could I go for so long and not remember them? This day, however, my mind was on other things. How long would it take me to get to the schoolhouse? Who would be there to greet me and show me where everything was? Would some of the children want to meet their new teacher and stop by to say hello before classes began? I was told it was a small country school but how many students attended? How many rooms would I have to live in? The questions were endless.

Three hours later, my car sat stalled by the side of the road, half on the road, and half in the ditch. No matter what I tried, the vehicle would not start. At first, I thought perhaps it had overheated so I sat inside and enjoyed a thermos lid of coffee that Mrs. Pike had insisted on sending with me. One truck stopped and asked if I needed any help but I assured him that the engine had overheated and I would be fine.

This was déjà vu for me. I couldn't help but think of my father's old car stalling in the Qu'Appelle Valley. This time, there was no valley, no old man named Winnipesaukee, only flat land for as far as I could see. Could there be homes behind the bluffs of trees that were scattered here and there? The truck that had stopped was long gone. Surely, there must be farms nearby. If my calculations were right, the schoolhouse couldn't be too far away - perhaps another hour's drive.

In one final attempt to get the motor running, I opened up the hood, pulled out every wire I could see, and plugged them back in again. I kicked the tire before getting back in. When I turned the key, the motor started up as if it had never skipped a beat.

"You and I are going to get along just fine, Molly," I said. "But you'd better start showing me more respect."

The name Molly slipped from my mouth before I realized what I'd said. It felt right though and even a bit comforting.

As I drove away, dust billowed out behind me and up the sides of the car. Somewhere, there were obviously minute openings in the chassis because it wasn't long before a layer of dust settled on the dashboard. I was sure there was a layer on my body too.

I came to a crossroads and saw in the southeast corner of the intersection, a small graveyard. According to the directions that the local school board (which I believe consisted of two people) sent to me, the little schoolhouse should be a mile west of that graveyard. I turned and saw in the distance a small bluff of trees on the north side of the road. The road now changed from gravel to dirt with deep ruts so with every bump and jerk, I thought my car was going to fall apart.

As I came closer to the bluff of trees, I saw that there was a building not too far off from the road. My heart was almost beating out of my chest with excitement. I pulled up in front, stopped in the middle of the road, and stared. Surely, this could not be the schoolhouse! My first thought was that it was an old abandoned granary.

At one time, the building must have been white but now most of the paint had peeled off, leaving the wood looking dull gray with white streaks and patches here and there. The steps going up to the door looked ready to collapse if anyone applied pressure on them. Two windows faced the front, one on each side of the door. They were large windows divided up into small panes. The window on the left had a piece of plywood nailed over the bottom half. The only slight indication that this might be a schoolhouse was the flagpole that stood in front that at one time, probably about the same time they'd built the school, had been painted white too. Now it sagged at an angle with the rope hanging down reminding me of a hangman's noose. I wasn't sure if that was a prophetic sign or not.

I backed up and turned into the driveway. I was still not convinced this was my final destination. Or, perhaps, hoping and praying that it wasn't. I drove up to the barbed wire gate, climbed out, pulled the wire loop off the post, and carried the fence to the side, letting it drop to the ground. As far as I could see there were no cattle grazing in the schoolyard. Perhaps the fence was more for keeping cattle out than keeping kids inside. The narrow dirt driveway led to a small barn farther into the bluff of trees. I stopped the car along the side of the building and got out.

"So, Molly," I said. "This might be our future home."

There was a weathered back door and a screen door that was banging against the side of the building. The screen was ripped and the door handle broken off. I cautiously stepped onto each step, waiting to see if it would hold my weight. They were stronger than they appeared.

I turned the handle and pushed the door open.

I was standing in what appeared to be living quarters. When the ad said there were small living quarters at the back of the school, they had left out one adjective 'extremely'. About seven feet in front of me was another door. I took two steps forward, opened it, and stepped into the classroom. Even though windows lined both sides of the room, it was still quite dim because no one had cared to wash the windows in a very long time.

I counted the desks. Ten all together and all the same size. Did that mean that a six-foot boy in grade eight had to try fit into the small desk, or did it mean that no one ever got to that grade? The teacher's desk was at the front of the room, facing the children. A blackboard covered the wall behind the desk and a large clock that wasn't working anymore, was attached to the wall right above the teacher's desk and almost touching the ceiling. Along the top of the blackboard, a teacher had printed the alphabet - the capital letters and the small.

Under the windows on the west side of the room was a long bookshelf, filled with books that had seen better days. Empty wooden apple crates sat against the wall under the windows on the east side. This I believed must be for the children to keep some of their supplies. An iron potbellied stove sat in the center of the room towards the back. From my schooldays, I knew this meant that the children who sat closest to it would be too hot and the ones closest to me would be freezing - as would I.

There was no separate entrance for a cloakroom when you came inside; you walked right into the room. There were hooks along the walls on both sides of the door, some were higher, and some lower. A wooden stand with a large glass water jug stood against the wall. From where I stood, I could see the dead bugs and cobwebs in the jug.

I had nowhere to begin. It was hard to imagine this was a functioning schoolhouse. With a sigh, I returned to the back room - my potential living quarters. I stood in the middle of the long narrow room and wondered what I was to do. Should I wait for someone to come to greet me? What if this wasn't the real school? What if they abandoned this one and built a new one not far away? Obviously, that was why there was the gate. No functioning schoolhouse is surrounded by a barbed wire fece!

Surely, that was the answer. With a sigh of relief, I went outside and climbed back into my car. I would drive down to the end of the mile road. I was sure the new school would be waiting there for me.

Well, *if* there was one, it wasn't visible to human eyes. I drove to the next mile road but saw nothing. I had to make certain though so I drove to the end another mile. There wasn't even a house in view. The sun was going down so I knew I might as well drive back from whence I'd come.

Perhaps things would look better in the morning.

Chapter Thirty Seven

Mrs. Pike, even over my protests, had packed a substantial lunch for me so I still had enough chicken sandwiches and potato salad to fill me up for my supper. After I'd eaten, gone to the outhouse, and washed my hands and face with ice cold water from the well, I curled up in the backseat of the car and went to sleep.

My last thoughts were of Molly. I wondered where we would be if she and I and our son were together. One thing I knew for sure; we would not be here in the middle of nowhere. We would probably be on her father's farm and that to me, would almost be worse. I fell asleep, thinking that life had thrown me some twists and turns but it was up to me to make the best of it. Perhaps living out here was the start of something good.

Someone, or something, banging and scraping against the car woke me. The car was rocking back and forth with such force, I was sure it was going to tip over. I thought I'd just fallen asleep but the sun was already getting high.

For a moment, there was silence. I hoped that whatever it was must be over but then there was a deafening crash against the side of the back door. When it stopped, I held my breath and slowly raised myself up. At the same time, a face appeared through the window staring at me. I'm not sure who was the most shocked.

A large mule deer with antlers that must have spanned five feet across stared at me, his eyes wild.

"Get out of here!" I yelled as loud as I could.

With a quick jerk of his head and another screeching scrape against my car window, he took off running.

I sat dazed for a few seconds. For the moment, all I could think about was my car door and I felt sick to my stomach. I pulled the handle down and pushed to open it. It would not budge. I scrambled out the other door and ran around to see how bad the damage was.

As soon as I saw it, I sank to the ground and burst into tears. I was not a tough young man who could take anything thrown at him; I was only a human who had at one point a breaking point and this was definitely one of those points.

I cried for the loss of Molly, my father, my grandfather, Winnipesaukee, and even little Toby, whom I knew I would never see again. I looked at the car, the dumpy old school house, my so-called lodging place, the dirty outhouse, the falling down barn, and cried some more. I wallowed in my self-pity for about twenty minutes. I would've been sitting on the ground wallowing longer but the sound of a car motor forced me back into reality.

The sound grew louder so I knew someone was driving into the yard. I jumped up, wiped my face with my shirttail, and knocked some of the dirt off my pants.

Fortunately, as the battered truck rounded the side of the building, dust billowed out from all sides of it. Now my eyes were burning and running, but it wasn't only from crying like a baby.

A man in his mid-forties emerged from the truck. He wore striped overalls worn thin at the knees, a red and black checkered flannel shirt with the sleeves rolled half way up his arm, rubber boots that still carried pieces of manure along the sides, and a dusty black felt hat. He sported a few days' growth on his weather beaten face and a toothpick stuck out the side of his mouth. He wouldn't have won a beauty contest but he looked friendly enough.

After one look at the bashed in car door and the scratches that ran almost from the front to the back, his eyes widened and he let out a low whistle.

"Old Andrew really got you good, didn't he? You can't leave that gate open."

I shook my head. "No, this was an old mule deer that did this. I was sound asleep when he woke me up, trashing my car."

"That'd be Andrew, son. He's been roaming these parts for years and for some reason, he's got a thing about vehicles." He walked over and ran his hand over the scratches, and then tried opening the door. He shook his head. "Well, I figure I can push that door back out so it will open and close." He looked back at me. "It ain't going to be very pretty though."

"Right now, sir, I'm not worried too much about being pretty. If you can get that door to open and close I'd be grateful."

"Yes, I can do that for you." The toothpick moved to the other side of his mouth. "Besides not forgetting to close that gate, hang some kind of red cloth over that ornament on your hood. We've discovered that he stays away if you do that. Not sure if the color matters but we've all started using red so we figure we'll stick with it. No one wants to wait and see if it makes any difference." He laughed when he said that and I could see that he had a stash of snuff in his cheek pocket. "By the way," he said, as he reached out his hand, "I'm Obadiah Johnson, but folks around here call me Obie."

We shook hands. His were hard and calloused and his shake was firm. My handshake was firm but I couldn't say my hands were the hands of a hard working man. I hoped he wouldn't judge me on my soft skin.

"I'm Patrick Smithson, sir. I have a teaching job somewhere in this area but this was the only school I could find. I hope it's all right that I parked here for the night."

"Of course, you can park here. This is now your school and your home. We want you to make yourself comfortable. Someone saw you driving up and down the road but we thought we'd give you time to rest up before we came to meet you." He went back to the truck and pulled something out from the seat.

He handed me a wicker basket with a clean cotton dishcloth covering the contents. "My wife wanted me to bring this to you. She figures a young bachelor doesn't know how to look after himself." He looked embarrassed. "Well, I hope you can use everything."

I took the basket from him and set it on the step. "Thank your wife. I do appreciate it. Will you have any children attending school here?"

He nodded. "Yeah, we have a son and daughter. Our daughter would've finished her grade four and our son would start grade six, if he passed."

"You mean you don't know if he passed or not? Those are provincial exams that the students take so you would know if he passed or not."

He laughed. "I guess if the teacher hadn't run off and disappeared, we might know."

I stared at him. "The teacher left before the year was out?"

He nodded. "Yep. Brought the kids to school one day and, lo and behold, no one was here. Gone. Of course, with the war on and everything, we couldn't find anyone to finish the year up for us."

"So, I'm finishing up last year's curriculum and then starting this year's?"

"Well, do the best you can. We're just pleased to have you." He gave me a quick once-over. "Something not right that the army didn't accept you?"

"No, sir. I'm sure I'm healthy enough. I chose to teach and not go to war. That's all."

I knew he was pleased to find a teacher but also a bit disappointed that I hadn't gone to war.

"So, Mr. Johnson, in the letter I received, it stated that classes were to commence the second week in September. September 12th. Is that still the case?"

"That's when they usually start but sometimes it depends on what's happening on the farm. If there's grain to get off, there's no way the farmers have time to take their kids to school."

I nodded. "Okay. I understand that. That's no problem."

"Well, just wanted to welcome you and hope you can get yourself all settled in. As soon as my crops are off, I'll have a look at that door on your car. Remember what I said about the red cloth on the hood. That'll keep Andrew away. Might be good to keep the gate closed too."

"I'll do that. Thank your wife for the basket. I appreciate it. By the way, how far away is the nearest store?"

"Not too far. Maybe twenty miles as the crow flies."

With that, he got back in his truck and backed out the driveway.

I lifted the cloth off the basket and saw jars of canned tomatoes, pickles, and jam. There was a bag of apples and one of potatoes and on top of everything was an apple pie.

I didn't realize how hungry I was until I saw that apple pie. However, the first thing I did was to take an old red bandana that the previous owner had left in the glove compartment and tie it around the hood ornament. I now realized the purpose of the bandana - it was to tie around one's nose and mouth to keep out the dust.

Since I was expecting to have a more furnished residence, I wasn't sure if I would even have a knife and fork for eating. I went inside, carrying my pie because if there were any more critters wandering about, besides the mule deer, I wasn't going to lose my treat.

This time, I took my time and looked around the room. The one and only window faced the backyard and under it was a small narrow table that did have a leaf that would pull out. The bed was at the end of the room and it fit exactly from one wall to the other wall. It was wide enough for one person. There was one chair at the end of the table. At the other end and close to the door was the slop pail. Thankfully, it was empty. A small narrow cupboard, which someone had painted dark green, with a cabinet above with one door, and several drawers below, was across from the table. I opened the door and saw that I was blessed with three chipped plates, two chipped cups, and one large cereal bowl, which was also chipped.

"At least everything matches," I said to no one. As the years passed, I discovered that I would carry on many conversations with myself.

In one of the drawers, I found my cutlery, which consisted of three forks, two butter knives, and four teaspoons. In the drawer beside it, there were spatulas, large knives for cutting bread and meat, and several large serving spoons.

A bucket and dipper sat on a small table on one side of the cupboard and on the other side of the cupboard was an old trunk. This, I assumed was where I would keep my clothes. It could also serve as a seat or a bedside table.

The only thing that seemed to be missing was a cook stove so I assumed that meant I would be cooking on top of the potbellied stove in the classroom. It was a good thing I didn't know how to bake anything.

I was beginning to understand why the former teacher had run off. This was going to be a definite challenge.

Everything in the room was clothed with a layer of dust. If southern Saskatchewan had anything in abundance, it was dust. It was the dustbowl of Canada.

I took out a fork from the drawer, wiped if off on my dusty pants, and plunged it into the apple pie. I had never tasted anything so wonderful in all my life. If it wasn't the most wonderful, it was right up there with Winnipesaukee's fried potatoes for sure.

For a few moments, I forgot that a large mule deer named Andrew had damaged my car, my students were far behind in their assignments and weren't even sure what grades they were in, and if I needed supplies, I would have to drive twenty miles as the crow flies. Since most roads aren't designed that way, I had a feeling it might be much longer.

I devoured the whole pie and wished I'd had more.

Chapter Thirty Eight

It took three days of working from early morning until late at night to get everything clean. I scrubbed and polished until my knuckles bled. I found some tools in a small shed behind the barn so I fixed the steps to the front and back doors. I removed the wood from the one front window only to see that the glass behind was gone so I had to nail it back up. I wasn't happy with that. The third day, I spent cleaning out the barn. Obviously, no one had removed the manure and old straw in a few years. It would make great fertilizer so decided that I would make one pile along the east side of the barn where the trees kept it hidden. Perhaps in the spring, I would have the class plant a garden.

The outhouse had a wasp's nest in one corner on the outside that I removed very carefully and the inside of the building was so full of bugs and spiders that the first thing I did was throw a bucket of water inside. Unfortunately, I forgot to remove the catalogues so I had to take them outside and let them dry in the sun. I was hoping it might soften the paper. I wondered what they would say if I asked for proper toilet paper. I had no idea what sort of budget they would give me. Since everything was rationed because of the war, the school board might think the children would waste the paper and that would cost money.

I tried to straighten the flagpole but the wood was so rotten, it crashed to the ground. I carried it around to the back and sawed it into one-foot lengths to use for kindling.

I spent the next two days pouring over the curriculum and trying to set up some sort of schedule. It wasn't easy when all I knew so far was that one child *might* be in grade four and one *might* be in grade six. By the end of the day, I had prepared a week's work for each day for grades one to eight. All the desks, the floor, and stove, were cleaned and polished. Every book was dusted and returned to a clean shelf even if the book was torn and falling apart.

The Friday before school was to commence, I made the trip into the closest town. It took me almost an hour to get there. It didn't help that I had to make several detours because the road suddenly came to an abrupt end. There was only one store so I didn't have many choices. I'm sure everyone in town knew within ten minutes that the new teacher was in town. Everyone was friendly and I appeared to be somewhat of a celebrity.

The morning that classes were to begin, I opened the gate and the front door of the schoolhouse early as I had no idea what time students would begin arriving. I felt it was as inviting as I could make it for what I had to work with.

September 12th came and went. There was no sign of any students. Did I have the date wrong? Each day I prepared for the beginning of the school year.

On the fourth day, I didn't bother to do anything. It was Friday so if any were coming, they would obviously be coming the next Monday.

I'd had my breakfast and was sitting on the back step drinking a cup of coffee when I heard the horn. I put my cup down and walked around to the front.

There, in the driveway, sat a truck. There were five girls crowded into the front seat with the driver and four boys in the box. One of the bigger boys jumped down when he saw me and opened the gate.

The driver, his head hanging out the window, yelled, "Is school on today?"

"Yes," I yelled back. "It started four days ago. Where was everyone?"

He shrugged. "No idea. Well, here's some for today" he said, as all nine children stood holding their lunch kits, in two rows in front of the truck. "What time should I pick them up?"

"I suppose four o'clock. That's when school lets out for the day."

He nodded, shoved the gearshift into reverse, and backed out onto the road, the motor whining.

So began my teaching career.

As they entered the classroom, the girls 'ooed' and 'awed' about how lovely it looked. I had gone into the woods for the first day of school and brought back a bouquet of fall flowers and some branches, each with different colored leaves. Some of the leaves were dropping off but they did look impressive sitting on the side of my desk.

The smallest girl, Christine, looked up at me wide-eyed and said, "It even smells good in here! It smells like a real school now. Not like it did before."

"How would you know that?" I asked, "This is your first year, isn't it?"

She nodded and grinned. "I used to come with my brother when my mom was busy."

I didn't even want to pursue that conversation but I was already considering making a few rules for parents. This was not a babysitting arrangement.

There were two in grade one - a boy named Adam and the girl named Christine. So far, grade two had the most students: Sandra, Martha, Fred, Sam, and Jeremy. The oldest boy, Edward, was starting grade six, and had a classmate, Hubert. Edward was as tall as I was and Hubert was the same height as Fred, who was in grade two.

As the day progressed, I began to realize what a staggering enterprise I had taken on. Only the girls knew their alphabet and even Christine could read but the boys were behind in everything. Edward stood awkwardly at the back of the room, not knowing what to do, because he couldn't fit in a desk.

"What did you do last year, Edward? Where did you sit?" I asked.

Before he could reply, one of the younger ones said, "He didn't come last year cause his pa died."

I looked at the boy standing in front of me. "I'm sorry, Edward. I didn't know." I looked around, trying to figure out what to do and how to handle the situation.

"When I came before," he said. "I could fit in a desk."

I looked at my desk. There was plenty of room at one end. Right now, the only thing filling the space was my pitcher filled with fall branches and flowers.

So I settled Edward at the end of my desk.

At almost noon, the door opened and an older woman stood inside the doorway with two boys that were definitely identical twins.

"I'm sorry we're so late," she said. "This is Jimmy and Johnny McKenzie. I'm Ida McKenzie, their grandmother."

I walked over, shook her hand, and introduced myself.

"And what grade are the boys in?" I asked.

She looked bewildered, "Oh goodness, I'm not sure. What grade are you boys in?"

The boys looked at her; then at each other, and I knew I was in trouble. Not only could I not tell one from the other, they were liars.

"Grade one," they said in unison.

Their grandmother looked at me. "They're not in grade one. I imagine about grade four. It's hard to know since the teacher last year left so suddenly." She gave them each a stern look and then looked back at me. "Don't let them get away with anything."

That I would learn as time went by was not an empty threat.

By the end of the day, I had thirteen students. Obie Johnson arrived with his two at noon. I had thirteen students and ten desks. Even with Edward sharing my desk, I was still short two desks. I couldn't very well put another person at the end of mine. The only solution I could find was to bring in the little table from my living quarters and let two students sit at that.

I put a child at each end of the table and gave each one an apple crate to sit on. It was a temporary solution and Mr. Johnson promised that he would check into finding some suitable desks and especially one for Edward.

Well, I survived that first day and was glad to have the weekend free. Free for what? It wasn't that I could go anywhere. To begin with, there was no place to go. My closest neighbor was at least three miles away which is not far at all but my second neighbor was six miles past that. It was also a busy time on the farms so it wasn't like I could pop by for a chat.

I occupied my time by doing more cleaning, going over the year's curriculum for the tenth time, and soaking in an old galvanized tub that I found up in the hayloft in the barn. I also began talking to myself aloud.

By the second weekend, it struck me that I might have to spend the whole winter holed up in this place so on the third weekend, I decided to drive to Swift Current, the nearest city. It took me close to three hours because of road conditions. I was either choking on dust on the dirt roads or praying a stray stone wouldn't shatter my windshield every time I met another vehicle on the gravel highway.

I was pleased to learn that the library would send out books for the children and when we were finished, we could pack them back up in their canvas bags and mail them back, postage paid. I was thrilled that I could borrow some for my own personal reading and that would help me get through the long cold winter months for many years to come. I also discovered to my delight that I didn't have to drive twenty miles, as the crow flies, to find a store and post office. There was a hamlet in the other direction that had both. And that was about all it had.

As I returned from the library, I saw a group of men standing around checking out the driver's side of my car.

One older man looked up when he saw me approaching and said, "I see Old Andrew got you good, son."

I could sense a touch of humor in his voice so I wasn't sure if the men were feeling empathy for me or thinking it was all a joke.

"This ain't nothing," an obvious farmer, by his smell, said. "You shoulda seen what he did to the side of my truck." He spread out his arms. "He made a gash from the headlight right to the tail light. Must've been a quarter inch deep. Then, to top it all off, he took to my wooden box and nearly ripped it right off the truck. Splinters all over the ground."

The other men roared.

"He did me twice," a younger man with dark hair that almost touched his shoulders, and wearing a dirty pair of overalls with holes in the knees, piped up. "After he tore into my truck, he went after my threshing machine and made his mark all along one side."

Again, everyone seemed to think that was funny.

"Why doesn't someone take out his shotgun and get rid of him?" I asked. "It sounds like he's wreaking havoc on all your vehicles and machinery."

Well, by the looks I received, you would've thought no one had ever heard the word 'shotgun' before.

"Son," the older man said, "We don't have much entertainment out here. You see how far apart we live from each other. The only thing we have to bring us a little excitement is trying to outsmart an old mule deer. Now if we up and shot him, he would be the winner."

"The winner of what?"

Four sets of blank eyes stared at me.

One of the men who had been quiet all this time, spoke up and said, "I know to a stranger this might seem silly but if you want to fit in, you have to come to understand Old Andrew."

They nodded in unison and walked away in four different directions.

Chapter Thirty Nine

L ife as a country schoolteacher in southern Saskatchewan in the early 1940s was anything but dull. The year began with thirteen students enrolled but by the end of November I had acquired two more.

We were in the middle of a grade three arithmetic class when the door burst open and a burly man wearing a thick parka, a fur cap, and high leather boots walked in. Two children followed close behind. Snow covered the ground so a cold sharp wind blew in with them. The room cooled off instantly.

"I have two children to join your school," he said. "We moved onto farm ten miles down main road. Can you teach them?" He had a loud deep voice and a heavy German accent.

I put down my book and walked over to shake his hand.

"Of course," I said. "What are their names and what grades are they in?"

"This is John, my son, and Ruth, my daughter. John is in grade three and Ruth is starting grade five."

"And what is your last name?"

"Brown. I am Aaron Brown."

The name didn't surprise me because so many German Canadians were changing their names to fit in or to escape persecution.

I smiled. "Don't worry, Mr. Brown, I'll get your children settled in right away. Can you pick them up at four?"

For the first time, he smiled. "Yah, be here at four."

Without another word, he went out, bringing in another gust of freezing air before slamming the door shut.

Now I had a real conundrum. Where was I to put two extra students? Both were extremely shy so it was difficult to get two words out of them and if I did, they spoke so softly, I could hardly hear what they said.

It didn't seem right to have the two sit on the floor for their first day of school and it wasn't fair to ask the others to give up their desks. The children themselves solved the problem.

Penelope raised her hand and said, "Ruth can share my desk if she'd like." And Edward who barely spoke two words in the day, said, "I think I could move over if John wants to sit beside me."

That solved the first problem of the day. It was a good thing that we had a supply of wooden apple crates. The second came a few hours later. It was almost three when I happened to glance out the window. It was starting to snow and the wind was picking up. I had a hard time seeing the gate into the schoolyard. I was hoping the parents would take note so they could come early to get the children.

By three thirty, a winter storm had arrived. Now I couldn't even see where the stump for the flagpole stood. I didn't want to panic but if no one arrived soon, those children would be here for the night or for however long the storm lasted.

Three days - that's how long the storm raged without letup. I was housebound with fifteen children. Two of whom I had met only hours before.

When I realized no one would be coming, in fact, no one was physically able to come; I decided to take action before darkness set in.

"Edward," I said. "You and I are going to remove the clothesline and attach it from the backdoor to the outhouse. Before we go to sleep tonight, each one of you will have to take his or her turn going there and it is easy to get lost if we can't see where we're going. Hubert and David, you will have to bring in as much firewood as you can and pile it up by the backdoor. Jimmy and Johnny, I want you to fill the galvanized tub with snow and put it on the stove because we'll need water. Everyone else, stay inside and don't venture out. Penelope, perhaps you can teach them some songs to sing."

By the end of the third day, I was ready to kick them all out and I didn't really care if they found their way home or not. Fortunately, the storm broke, the sun shone, and when I looked outside a few hours later, I saw one sled and one hay wagon lined with straw, each pulled by a team of horses, come into the driveway. I shouted for joy.

"Children," I said, "I believe your chariots await you."

No one even asked what a chariot was because each one was as happy to see the end of me as I was to see the end of them. They were in their coats and out the door in record time. Aaron Brown, driving the hay wagon, got down and met me at the door, carrying a gunnysack that was bulging with something.

"My wife sent this," he said. "You have fed our children for three days so I don't think you have much left. We are sorry we burden you so soon as we meet."

I laughed. "I hope it wasn't too traumatic for your children. And, no, I don't have much food left. Another day and we would have been eating snow." I took the sack from his hand. "Please thank your wife for me. I would like to meet her some day."

"I'm sorry," he said. "She doesn't speak English very good."

"Okay but make sure to thank her."

He nodded and started to walk away.

"Mr. Brown," I said. "If your wife would like to learn English, I can send some books home with the children for her. Perhaps they can help her."

"That would be very kind, Teacher. I know she would like that."

When I opened the sack and pulled out all the food, I couldn't help feeling how fortunate I was. It had been a trial for me but I felt that I had passed. There was enough food to last me for a week.

The next week when Obie Johnson came to pick up his children, I tried to explain that I now had fifteen students and still only ten actual desks. Even though commendable, the children who offered to share their space with the newcomers needed the room for themselves. The only place left was the floor and it was not proper for children to have to sit on their coats on the floor. Not only was it uncomfortable, the floor was cold and it was not healthy.

"I'll see what I can do, Patrick," he said. "I can't guarantee real school desks but maybe we can come up with something."

Three days later, he arrived with an old wooden kitchen table and three chairs piled in the back of his truck. I was elated. It was now a full room. I pushed my desk over against the west wall so the new table could fit beside mine. Now we had three children at the table, ten children at proper desks, and two sitting on apple crates at the table taken from my living quarters.

Of course, when I say I had fifteen registered students, that didn't guarantee how many I would have in class. In the fall during harvest or in the spring during seeding, I might have five because the others weren't able to get a ride to school or they were working in the fields. However, if the parents were busy but the children had a ride to school, I might end up with three or four little brothers and sisters. I was not exactly pleased with the situation but it turned out to be a blessing at times because the older ones, girls especially, loved to play school so I would have them sit at the back of the room conducting their own classes.

It worked fine until one day Penelope approached me as I was trying to teach the grade two students their multiplication tables. Out of the five, I had only three that day.

"Mr. Smithson," she said, "there's something wrong with the children today. They won't answer any of my questions or even draw pictures. They seem really afraid of something and I don't know what I'm doing wrong." Tears welled in her eyes. "I think they're all afraid of me."

The tears in her eyes overflowed down her face and she started sobbing. I looked over at the three little girls and one boy who should not have been at the school to begin with, and I could see they looked terrified.

I walked over.

"What's the matter, children? Are you afraid of something?"

The small boy who could very well have been still wearing a diaper, pointed to Penelope and nodded.

"You're afraid of Penelope?"

All four nodded vigorously.

"Why?"

I noticed one of the girls glancing in another direction so I quickly followed her gaze. Fast enough to see Johnny McKenzie with his head down and a smirk on his lips.

"What did Johnny tell you?"

Everyone's eyes got big but no one said anything.

"It's okay. You can tell me. Should I be afraid too?"

The little boy nodded and whispered, "Penelope carries a snake in her pocket and if we talk to her, she'll let it out to bite us."

"And did Johnny tell you that?"

They all nodded vigorously.

That was the last time Penelope had any trouble because every time she had her own little class at the end of the room, Johnny spent his class time sitting in the corner.

By the spring of that first year, I had learned most of the ins and outs of teaching in a one-room schoolhouse. I learned to deal with chimney fires, runaway horses, boys dropping toads down the back of girls' dresses, girls refusing to talk to other girls, boys fighting behind the barn, boys kissing girls behind the barn, and children throwing up over my shoes. The one thing I never did learn was how to handle the parents.

"I don't think you're being entirely fair here, Patrick," one father said to me when he found out that his son was not making the progress that was expected of him.

"What do you mean? I'm being very honest. Fred is not working up to his potential. He spends most of the time whispering or doodling on books. If he wants to go into the next grade, he has to start taking this seriously."

I didn't see Fred for the next two weeks so I figured either his father didn't want me to teach him anymore, or he'd beaten the poor boy so badly, he didn't dare show up at school.

When Fred finally returned, I decided to continue as if nothing had ever happened, and perhaps nothing had because Fred was caught up in all his schoolwork, and had a completely different attitude. In fact, when I left that little school, Fred was one of my most outstanding students.

There was also a matter of morals. Sometimes it's difficult, actually impossible, for a teacher to know what to say in certain situations.

It was in the spring. School was almost out for the year and everyone was already talking about their summer vacations. This day, Obie brought seven of the children to school in his truck. Hubert, now almost fourteen, drove a horse and buggy and brought the McKenzie boys, Martha, and Fred. He had no trouble removing the harness and putting the horse in the barn for the day, forking in some hay for her, and filling up the water trough.

Parents took turns bringing the rest of the children. The only one who brought his children every day with the horse and wagon was Aaron Brown.

"Hubert," I said one day as he was leaving and the Brown children were standing out by the road waiting for their father, "you go right by the Brown farm. Why don't you take John and Ruth? You still have room in your buggy."

Hubert's face turned red and for a moment, he didn't know what to say.

He fidgeted with the reins for a moment and then said, "Well, I think their dad is on his way now so there's no point."

"That's true but you should see if your folks can't make some arrangement with him. It seems foolish for both of you to come separately when you live so close, don't you think?"

Without making eye contact, he nodded and clucked at his horse to move. They went out of the yard and I watched from the side of the schoolhouse. Both Brown children kept their heads down and none of the children in the buggy waved goodbye. Was this something that I'd missed? Usually, I was so busy making sure everyone was out of the schoolroom, that I never paid much attention to what they did after that.

In about ten minutes, Mr. Brown showed up and the children left for home.

That night as I lay in bed, my thoughts as always turned to Molly. I wondered how she would have liked living out here with no close neighbors, trying every day to show the children how important an education was, and listening to them talk about the war and whose father or cousin or brother hadn't come back. At times, I wondered too how important an education was. There were no jobs for anyone. Even patients were paying their doctors with chickens and milk. One store in Swift Current was willing to trade merchandise for poultry or anything else a farmer had to offer.

Then the rains came and it boosted everyone's feelings. The war was in full swing and suddenly there were more jobs helping with the war effort. Swift Current was soon to become a bustling city again.

But I knew not all was right in my little part of the world. It came to a climax one day when Aaron Brown arrived at the school the same time as Hubert Seaman's father. I felt it was a good time to get the two together and make some better arrangements for picking up the children. Usually Hubert came to school with the buggy but since this day his father came, it couldn't have been a better time to make a suggestion.

"Mr. Seaman," I said, "Don't you think it would be a good idea if you and Aaron Brown took turns bringing and picking up the children? It seems like such a waste of your time now that you're so busy with seeding. Usually Hubert has the buggy so that would free both of you men up. What do you think?"

Mr. Seaman stared at me with as much loathing as I'd ever seen in one man's face - almost as much as the hatred Jacob Jordan showed for me.

"I don't have anything to do with Nazis," he hissed, in a low voice.

I stared at him. "Nazis? Mr. Brown isn't a Nazi. He's a Canadian. He's a farmer the same as you."

266

"He can't even speak proper English. His wife can't speak any. If you're a Canadian, you speak English."

"Really? Your name sounds more German than his does, Mr. Seaman. Or, should I say Siemens? I imagine that your parents and grandparents spoke German too."

His eyes blazed. "My name is Seaman. It is not Siemens. I know what you're trying to say."

I shrugged. "I know what it is now but I was told your family changed it."

At this point, all attention was on Mr. Seaman and me. I knew I shouldn't say too much because of the children but I couldn't stop myself. We did not need the war carrying over to our part of the country.

"That had nothing to do with me. I am Canadian and nothing else."

"Mr. Brown has changed his name too. It used to be Braun. So you are both the same."

"But we adjusted. We changed."

"So you think just because a person speaks German and still has an accent that makes that person a Nazi?"

"No but he has his own ways." He shoved his hands into his pockets and glared at me.

"Everyone has their own ways. That is what makes us people. What will you do when the war is over? Will you stop hating him then?"

At this, Aaron Brown spoke up. "It is all right, Mr. Smithson. I don't want trouble. We will stay as we are. I will bring my children on my own. It's better that way." He smiled. "But thank you."

He turned his horses round and headed in the direction of home. Mr. Seaman waited a few minutes before getting into his truck and then followed him. He never looked back but the children in the back of the truck waved and smiled as they drove away.

I waved back and hoped that when those children became adults, they would look beyond color or nationality but see each person as to what they were on the inside.

The next fall, before school was in session, the Browns moved south across the border into the United States and I never heard whatever happened to them. Before they left, however, they stopped by the school one Saturday afternoon. Mrs. Brown came to the back door carrying the books I'd lent her in one hand and freshly baked apple strudel in the other.

With a slight German accent, she said, "Thank you, Teacher, for helping me to learn English."

"You're very welcome," I said. "I hope the war will be over soon and life will be easier for you and your family."

That was the last time I saw them.

In the second year, I finally attended my first teachers' conference in Moose Jaw. Not that it was a personal invitation - Obie Johnson found out about it and said that I should qualify to go. I was thrilled but as it turned out, many didn't actually accept me as a 'real' teacher.

"But," as one pompous university graduate and speaker told me, "It's good to have young men filling in for the time being. The war will be over soon and there will be other jobs for you, I'm sure."

At the time, my nose was a little out of joint. I knew that I was working harder than most. On the other hand, perhaps I should have been grateful. It was the jolt that I needed, forcing me to think about attending Normal School. I knew I really didn't want to spend the rest of my life where I was. And as the man said, after the war, there would be plenty of real teachers looking for work.

What would happen to the children though? If I left, where would they find someone to take my place? No one in their right mind would want to teach in a one room falling-apart school with a tiny sleeping space in a back room.

I never did attend another Teacher's Conference while teaching at that school. After three years, I approached Obie one day in early spring and said that I would like to leave and finish my training in Moose Jaw at the Normal School for teachers.

He sat quietly for several seconds and then said, "And then you would come back?"

I shook my head. "No, Mr. Johnson, I think it's time for me to move on. I'm sure you can find someone to take my place."

"No, we will never find anyone to take your place, Patrick. Do you think anyone would want to come out here and live in the middle of nowhere? We don't even have a proper place for anyone to live."

I stared at him. "I came here. That doesn't say much for me, does it?"

He laughed. "That says a lot for you. You were willing to put yourself out. You were willing to live in terrible conditions and teach in a school that didn't have proper books or even desks. Where would we ever find another person with such a big heart and be so dedicated? No, we won't find anyone like you again. The children think the world of you and they have learned so much." He paused and then pleaded, "Won't you reconsider?"

"No, I think this will be my last year here. I'm sorry, Obie."

Three weeks later, Obie Johnson and Henry McKenzie dropped by in the evening. It was a beautiful evening, the sun was beginning to set, and the song of birds filled the air. The occasional bellow of a cow somewhere in the pasture a mile or so behind the schoolyard could be heard as they headed home for milking. The land was so desolate that I discovered sounds travelled for miles. It's true it was lonely and seemed so empty but somehow there was an awesome beauty to it all. The land reminded man how small he really was.

I heard the sound of Obie's old truck before it reached the yard. I waited on the front step while enjoying my after dinner cup of tea. Both men emerged from the truck with smiling faces so I knew something was up.

"We have some great news for you, Patrick." Henry was the first to speak.

I stood up to greet them. After shaking their hands, I asked, "And what might that be? You've found a teacher to take my place?"

They looked at each other like two small schoolchildren who had been holding back a great secret.

"Well, no," Obie said, "but we are going to let you attend Normal School. The School Board will pay your fee and when you come back, you will have a brand new school to teach in."

"And," added Henry, "You will get a raise."

They both looked at me with such hope and expectation in their eyes, what choice did I have?

However, rethinking it, I realized I should have threatened them much sooner.

Normal school was enjoyable but somewhat disappointing. The attendance was staggering - suddenly over nine hundred young women and men wanted to enter the teaching field. My teaching experience helped me a great deal and there weren't too many things that were new to me. I noticed that much of it did not have anything to do with *what* to teach but more about knowing *how* to teach. For example, they emphasized how important it was for children to be educated. I soon realized that not everyone had a burning desire to teach small children or even to be teachers, so the Normal teachers had their work cut out for them. They did their best to try to ooze with enthusiasm and dedication and then hoped it would rub off.

Much of the course was about things I'd already practiced and mastered in my small schoolhouse. It seemed more plain common sense to me. For example, for over an hour a lively middle-aged woman taught us when it was best to open windows and when it was best to keep them closed; a distinguished male teacher with silver hair and matching neatly trimmed beard, explained how much coal or wood it would take to keep a one room country school warm in winter. Then, there were the necessary things we had to know; like how to teach children with no talent to draw or how to form a choir without any musical instrument. One whole afternoon was spent learning how to decorate a classroom for the various celebrations during the year.

There were some highlights though. An older teacher invited several of us to his home one evening to discuss topics that would never be discussed as part of our curriculum. He took an interest in me because he realized that I'd undertaken more than most of the others would ever have to - and without any formal training. Often as he spoke, he would ask my opinion.

I remember one lively discussion we had in his living room. There were about ten of us there. It was a chilly evening in March and we were all looking forward to soon getting our diplomas. Mr. Martin lived on North Hill as it was called, in a three-story brick house with a turret along the north side of the building. In my opinion, it seemed a perfect type of home for an educator. We had enjoyed coffee and some cookies while making light conversation. There were usually a few who had comical experiences to share and our host didn't seem to mind if they included some of his colleagues. I wasn't sure if Mr. Martin had ever been married or if he'd always been a bachelor but education was the only thing he talked about.

"So, Patrick," he said, during a break in the conversation. "How well do you communicate with the school board and the trustees where you teach? Have they always been cooperative?"

I placed my cup on a small table beside me and said, "I guess they have been as best they can."

"What do you mean by that? Do you always have everything you need for teaching or have you gone without?"

"Without what, sir? If you don't mind me asking?"

He threw up his hands and said, "Well, let's take an extreme example. Do all the students have a desk?"

"Well, they do now. Not that they're real desks, mind you. I had fifteen students and only ten desks."

There were several gasps and giggles.

"Really? And how did you improvise?"

Before I could reply, he said, "This is what I'm talking about, class. This is real teaching in a small country school. Amazing! So, Patrick, how do you handle the situation?"

So I described how my students sat at desks and tables and since there weren't enough chairs, they sat on apple crates.

Mr. Martin was thrilled. He clapped his hands. "That's the spirit. You must learn to improvise. But now you come to the second step. It is time to get your proper desks. What do you do?"

Most of the ones present knew you had to go to the local school board or the school trustees.

"Aw, so, Mr. Smithson, when you begin your new school year, what are you going to do? Are you going to go to the school trustee and voice your concerns?"

"I don't think I'll have to, sir. The school board has paid for my tuition here and when I go back, I will have a brand new schoolhouse, new desks, and a raise in pay."

He stared at me. "A new school? A raise? How did you manage that?"

"I said I was leaving."

Mr. Martin burst out laughing.

He stood up and said to the group of student teachers, "And now you know how to deal with the school board and the trustees." He snickered about that for the next ten minutes.

We returned to Mr. Martin's house for more discussions before the term ended. The topics were varied. One young woman wanted to know what to do if one of the male students turned amorous towards her. This brought on some chuckling and whispering.

"Don't laugh," Mr. Martin said. "This happens quite often. You must always be aware of the situation. Even standing too close to a fifteen year old boy at the blackboard can get a young boy's hormones racing."

"What if there's a big bully who decides to beat up the teacher?" a rather fragile male student asked.

So the topics went on. We learned from each other and listened to Mr. Martin's sage advice.

It was with sadness when we had to say goodbye and go our separate ways.

So I taught for five more years in that brand new schoolhouse, built on the exact spot where the old one had sat, and I lived in a small cabin at the back of the property. I now had a cook stove, a real bed with a mattress in a separate room, and even an icebox to keep my food cold - as long as Edward remembered to bring ice to me every day from the ice house at his farm. I made it a point not to complain about the sawdust he left behind all over the kitchen floor. I especially appreciated that icebox because one of the new students whose family was trying to get into the dairy business would bring me a quart of milk every other day. Now, I could skim off the cream and have real cream in my morning cup of coffee.

That new student was a young woman named Rachael. She was seventeen and a beautiful girl. It was the first time since Molly that something stirred within me. It was a feeling that I knew I had to suppress but Rachael did not make it easy. Sometimes I would look up from my desk at the class and she would be gazing at me with those beautiful green eyes and with a shy smile on her lips. I kept my distance for many weeks but one day, I had to run back to my cabin before classes began to get something. When I opened the door, Rachael was standing there. I would like to say she was not waiting for me and that it was purely by accident that we ran into each other but I knew it was not. The quart of milk that she brought had already been in the icebox for ten minutes. No, she was waiting for me.

"Oh, Mr. Smithson," she said, with a voice that was as smooth as silk, "I was having trouble with the door on the icebox. Do you think you could make sure it's shut? Mama would be dreadfully upset if your milk turned sour on you. She would blame me as sure as anything."

I tried to smile and sound natural. "I'm sure it will be okay, Rachael. You go to class. School starts in five minutes." I laughed but it sounded hollow in my own ears. "Your mama might be more upset if you were late for school."

"Don't worry about that. We can go in together, Patrick." It was then I noticed the top three buttons on her dress were undone and I was staring at more than I should've been seeing. Unfortunately, she saw me staring too.

Without saying another word, she moved toward me. I stood like a dead man. Her arms went around my neck and her lips pressed against mine. I tried to push her away but perhaps it was half an attempt on my part. It was a fiery kiss that sent a shiver through my whole body. I knew this was all wrong but I could not stop.

Even in that heat of the moment, I thought I heard someone whispering my name.

I pulled my lips away and whispered her name, "Molly."

Rachael stared at me and before I knew it, up went her hand and it flew against my face with such a force, I thought my head might fly off. However, that slap brought me to my senses.

The rest of the day was a blur. I couldn't bring myself to look at Rachael and several children asked if I was not feeling well. That evening I telephoned Obie Johnson and explained what had happened. I was prepared to forsake my teaching profession forever.

"She really slapped you that hard, did she?" he asked.

"Yes, she did. I swear, Obadiah, I cannot believe how forward this girl can be. I do understand the circumstances though and I know I won't be allowed to teach anymore. You can let the others on the board know and I can even leave tonight if you like."

"It's Friday," he said. "I'll get back to you sometime on the weekend."

All weekend I felt sick. I kept busy by cleaning my cabin, washing clothes, and starting to pack. If I had to leave, I wasn't going to stay a minute longer than I had to. Shame washed over me like scalding water filled with bleach. I deserved everything they would hand out. My reputation as a teacher was forever ruined. Reports about my conduct would spread across the country. Perhaps, my only option would be to move south, across the border.

By late Sunday afternoon, I began packing up the car. Obadiah Johnson had kept his word and tried to fix the damage Old Andrew had caused but it still didn't look very good. It did open and shut though so I was happy for that. The red bandana on the hood ornament was now more of a pink than red but it seemed to work at keeping the old mule deer away.

It was almost eight when Obie drove into the yard and parked in front of the cabin.

He looked over and saw the backseat of my car almost filled to the brim with boxes.

"What are you doing, Patrick?"

A bit embarrassed, I confessed, "I thought I might as well get a head start."

"A head start for what?"

"Leaving. That's what I'll have to do, right?"

He shook his head. "You're not going anywhere. We were over visiting Rachael's folks." He waited a few seconds before continuing. "She's pregnant, did you know?"

I stared at him. "Pregnant? She kissed me two days ago. That's all that happened. She can't be pregnant."

Obie roared. "Not from you. From the young fellow who works at Murphy's store. Her folks are sending her away to have this baby and then she's giving it up for adoption. At least, that's the plan her parents have for her. It sounds like the girl has a mind of her own and she's been a heap of trouble ever since she turned thirteen. I don't think anyone knows about this advance she made on you, so there shouldn't be any gossip. The gossip will center round the girl going away to have a baby. So, you can unpack and put everything back where it belongs."

The incident did two things for me. I was better prepared for dealing with young women students and more conscious of my own behavior, making sure I always stayed professional. Even then, as the years went by, I

278

became aware of a few student crushes. It also made me aware of something else. Molly would always be on my mind. Until the day that I could completely move on, I could not give my whole soul to another woman.

When I did decide to leave, they had no problem finding a new teacher. The road in front of the school was now graveled and if there were any emergencies, there was a telephone in the teacher's private office.

Within the next few years, along with the telephone poles came electricity. Then, school buses arrived. Sadly, I heard that because the attendance became so low, all the children were going to be bused to the school in town. That meant some children had to get up before dawn and in the winter months, would return home in the dark too. This, of course, was called progress.

Chapter Forty

I always kept in mind Winnipesaukee's advice about teaching boys; however, it turned out that although I searched for a boys' school, there were none to be found that wouldn't take me far away from where Molly was buried. So, after teaching at several different schools, I headed back from whence I came. My first stop was to visit Mr. and Mrs. Pike.

The years hadn't been kind to them. They didn't farm anymore because both of them were crippled up with arthritis so they rented the land and had just enough money to get by on.

"We have food on our plate, Patrick, and a roof over our head," Mr. Pike said, as he tapped his pipe on his teeth.

Mrs. Pike added, with a smile, "It's a leaky roof but it's all we've got."

I shared a meager meal with them and said I would be back as soon as I'd settled in to the teacher's residence.

"You're going to be teaching school in town here?" Mrs. Pike said, her eyes lighting up. "That's wonderful."

I smiled. "Yes, it seems they were in need of a principal so I applied for the job."

Mr. Pike laughed. "A principal? And imagine, the last time you were here you were spending every hour over at that table studying to be a teacher. I'm proud of you, son."

After I'd settled in and before meeting the staff or anything else, I asked around about someone who was good at fixing leaky roofs. I contacted the company and asked them to have a look at the Pike's roof and then give me an estimate. For an extra hundred dollars, they were willing to drop what they were doing and start working at the Pike's farm. The elderly couple were beside themselves.

"Patrick, we have to pay you back. We can't let you waste your money on the roof of this old house." Mrs. Pike was quite adamant.

"You can pay me back," I said. "I'll be wanting a few home cooked meals for the next few years and I intend to get them here."

I made many trips out to that farm until one day, I received a phone call that Mr. Pike had suffered a heart attack and was with us no more. For the next few days, I helped Mrs. Pike find suitable lodging and arranged to have their land put up for sale. She didn't last much longer after that. I would go over to the seniors' home after school was over most days and have a cup of tea with her. When she passed away, I was shocked when her lawyer called me in and told me that all her assets had been willed to me. My bank account was growing and I still hadn't spent the money from selling the farm.

During the spring break that year, I made a trip up north. It was time for me to put a decent headstone on my father and grandfather's graves. It was not a lighthearted trip but it was one that I had to do. It took three days to have the headstones made so I spent my time driving around the area.

Most of the old neighbors were gone. They said that the Beckers had both died. Alvin Becker died first and his wife tried burying him out in the back pasture but the ground was too hard so she was forced to ride horseback to the train station. She never did learn to drive and the horseback ride almost did her in. She was rushed to the hospital but passed away a few days later.

Henry Yake also died from a heart attack. He was delivering groceries when they found his car in the ditch but it was too late to revive him. There was a new couple at the train station but very few people were catching the train anymore. The steam engine was replaced by the diesel years back so there wasn't much of a need to even stop. Once a week there was a train taking supplies up to the far north and it would blow its whistle as it flew past doing sixty miles an hour.

The log house on the old homestead had stood empty for many years but now it stood all alone with not one tree surrounding it. Brush cutters had cleared the land years before. A crop of wheat surrounded the house and the one shed that was still standing.

I pulled into the driveway and walked up to the house. There wasn't a gate to open anymore. The wheat must have been fall wheat because it was green and up a few inches now. I walked to the door and tried opening it. At first, I thought it was locked but I pushed and it opened. The kitchen table stood in the middle of the room with two chairs on each side. There were cups on the table and an ashtray over flowing with butts. I walked into the living room. It was bare except for the old couch that didn't look much worse than I'd seen it years before. The two bedrooms were empty of everything so someone must have wanted the beds. The air smelled dusty and stagnant.

I left the house and walked up the slight mound to see if the graves were still there. The little fence was gone and so were the markers my father had put there. The trees were gone, the markers were gone, and all I could see as far as I looked were rows of wheat.

At least the RCMP had buried my father and grandfather in a decent graveyard. It was along the main road beside a small church that no one had attended for many years. Someone came to cut the grass in the summer but that was all the upkeep it received. Now families buried their loved ones in city or town graveyards. Personally, I liked the small graveyard where my father and grandfather slept. All together, there were perhaps twenty graves. Some had large marble stones but most were like the ones I brought - small but adequate and I knew if the ones under the ground could see them, they would be pleased. Neither my father nor grandfather believed in spending foolishly, and a grand gravestone would have been wasted money in their minds.

And yes, I did stop at Sarah's valley on my way home.

Tall grass and wild roses filled the spot where Winnipesaukee's cabin once stood. There was no sign that anything had ever filled that space before. The ramshackle shed was gone and the dugout into the hill for storing food in summer was so overgrown with grass and weeds that if you didn't know it had been there, you would never know it had ever existed.

And yes, I searched for the gold nuggets that Winnipesaukee had hidden. I couldn't control my curiosity. School wasn't starting for another eight days so what was I to do? This was not only giving me something to occupy the days, it was therapeutic also. I had been so busy the past years, that I hadn't taken the time to evaluate my life. What was I doing? Was I contributing to society? What were my goals? Could I make a difference to those children that were under my care for more hours in the day than they were with their parents?

And yes, I found Winnipesaukee's treasure. After I'd dug up under almost every old evergreen, my spade hit something hard. I dug around it and pulled it out. It was a small metal container, that at one time, had probably held chewing tobacco. With a wildly beating heart, I opened the tin. Just as Winnipesaukee said in his Will, there were three large gold nuggets inside.

What did I do? Well, I kept it in my bureau drawer for a few years. I wasn't sure if I should make an attempt to find some of Winnipesaukee's family and if so, where was I to begin. Obviously, the place to start was to have the nuggets analyzed by an assayer. If they were worth a large sum of money, I would have to track down Tobias Lawdry somehow. For all I knew, that little boy could be anywhere in the world. I was sure nothing would hold him down to one place.

The results came back quickly.

"Go to the top drawer, Michael, and bring out the metal box. Take the nuggets out and hold them in your hand."

The old man smiled as he watched Michael Lawdry lift the lid, carefully pick up each nugget, and hold them in the palm of his hand. He stared down at them for a few seconds and then returned them to the box.

He looked at Patrick with raised eyebrows. "They're iron pyrite, aren't they?"

Patrick nodded. "I'm afraid so. Fool's gold."

He held out his hand and Michael handed him the box. Patrick looked inside before closing the lid.

With a chuckle, he said, "I often wonder if the woman he stole them from knew what it was." He shrugged. "Maybe she was conning people with it. Who knows? She was a wicked woman so maybe she played a trick on the young man named Frank Lawdry. If so, I'm glad that he never found out. He died thinking that he had a hidden treasure and that he'd got one over on his wife."

Patrick Smithson handed the box back to Mr. Lawdry.

"These I give to you, Michael. They will be a reminder of your ancestors and of the long story that an old man who once knew Frank Lawdry told you. Besides, they really are your inheritance."

Michael smiled. "Thank you, Patrick. I will cherish it." He stood up and buttoned his coat. The wind was once again howling around the corners of the building. He dreaded going back out into the cold. However, he could see that Patrick was tired and he needed his sleep. His flight was leaving from Regina the next afternoon so he would have to head back home.

"Could I come and have breakfast with you in the morning, Patrick?"

The elderly man answered, "You are welcome to join me." He grinned. "Perhaps, we can get Karen to bring us breakfast in my room."

Michael laughed. "Just make sure you have your afternoon coffee after I'm gone. Let me know if she doesn't bring it for you." He handed the old man his business card. "Here's my address and phone number. We must keep in touch, Patrick."

Tears glistened in Patrick's eyes.

"Oh, Michael, I almost forgot. I have something for you." He reached for an envelope on his desk and handed it to him. "My will is already made up and my lawyer knows exactly what it entails; however, could you make sure my *wishes are carried out? I have no family and I'm afraid that after I'm gone, people won't understand. You've heard my story so I know you will."*

"Of course, I'll look after it for you." He bent down and hugged the old man. "Don't forget we're having breakfast in the morning and I'll come to visit whenever I can, Patrick."

"Thank you, Michael Lawdry."

Margaret was working the late afternoon shift that day so before she left, she stopped at Patrick's door. It was eleven o'clock so she knew he would be asleep but he was one resident that she liked to check on before leaving for home.

She quietly opened the door and peeked in. She was surprised to see his bedside lamp was still on.

"Patrick Smithson," she said, trying to sound authoritative, "you should be sleeping now. All this excitement has kept you up, hasn't it?"

She walked over to the bed.

Patrick was lying back against two pillows, his eyes were closed, and he was smiling.

Margaret stood looking down and let the tears flow.

"Oh, Mr. Smithson, I'm so sorry to see you go." She wiped a tear away and reached down to hold his hand. "I will miss you. You were a special friend."

Michael was unable to attend the funeral but two weeks later, he returned to Patrick's town. The day he arrived, the sun shone and the temperature rose to above normal. The snow sparkled in the sunshine and he could imagine the old man sitting at his window looking out over the vast prairie. There was no need to stop at the Home so he drove straight to the cemetery. Just as Patrick had done many times before, Michael walked past row after row of graves until he saw the gravestone he was looking for. He was pleased to see that someone had taken care of Patrick's last wishes and had buried his ashes where he had wanted them buried.

Before reading the engraving, he reached into his pocket, removed a small metal box, and scattered the crushed contents over the gravesite. The flash of gold caught the eye of a caretaker standing not far away and he heard the well-dressed man say, "Here's to a man who was anything but a fool. It was an honor meeting you, Patrick Smithson."

He then bent down and read the inscription on the new gravestone.

Here in this spot lies
Molly Ann Smithson, wife of Patrick Smithson, and daughter to Jacob and Martha Jordan.
Born: 1921   Died: 1938
Baby Boy Smithson. Born: 1938 Died: 1938
Patrick Smithson, beloved husband to Molly.
Born: 1919 Died: 2014
Ya ni go we ya. Ni go we

The End

If you enjoyed this book, please post a review on your favorite retailer's website.

Books by Sharon Mierke

The Beryl Swallows mystery series

Virtual Enemies Book 1
Case Closed...Not Book 2

The Mabel Wickles mystery series

Deception by Design..Book 1
Calamity by the Carwash
Cold Case Conundrum
Frozen Identity

Historical Fiction

Sarah's Valley
Return to Sarah's Valley
The Widow's Walk

SHARON MIERKE

SHARON MIERKE

Made in the USA
Coppell, TX
06 October 2022